CUSTOMER
SERVICE
EXCELLENCE
UK
The Government Standard

Kent
County
Council

D0309758
C333710633

SIMON AND SCHUSTER

First published in Great Britain in 2015 by Simon and Schuster UK Ltd
A CBS COMPANY

1 3 5 7 9 10 8 6 4 2

Simon & Schuster UK Ltd
1st Floor,
222 Gray's Inn Road
London WC1X 8HB

Simon & Schuster Australia, Sydney
Simon & Schuster India, New Delhi

A CIP catalogue record for this book
is available from the British Library.

PB ISBN: 978-1-47111-579-0
Ebook ISBN: 978-1-47111-580-6

Printed and bound by CPI Group (UK) Ltd, Croydon, CR0 4YY

www.simonandschuster.co.uk
www.simonandschuster.com.au

To Pastor Matthew Norris, the funniest, most mischievous minister to ever come out of Warrington

ONE

Heroes and Villains

School's out for summer, as a mad-man in make-up once sang. It was the first day of the holidays and six weeks of sunstroke, mindless mayhem and misadventure lay ahead. It truly felt like anything could happen, the world our playground. Who knew what scrapes and hi-jinks awaited us? As it happened, it wasn't Enid Blyton who penned what was to come. It felt more like Stephen King had seized our world and turned it upside down.

I should probably help you get up to speed. My name is Will Underwood, and I'm a ghost. Not some freaky-deaky, spooky-ooky, malevolent spirit-type thingie, I should add. I'm the same nice guy I was before I died, only now I'm hopeless at ping pong, pottery and playing pattycake. Being an ethereal free-roaming vapour really does put a dampener on the everyday shenanigans one takes for granted. The only person who can see me is my best friend, Dougie Hancock. Poor lad. The night I died, he lost a friend and gained a phantom. You see, I haunt Dougie; wherever my pal goes, I follow. We're mates through thick and thin, through life *and* death.

That first day of the summer break saw Andy Vaughn, Dougie and I hit the town and our local haunts (pardon the expression). The comic shop got hammered, the lads picking up their latest issues of essential superhero reading: *The Walking Dead*, *Hellboy* and whatever the latest incarnation of *Spider-Man* was. We loitered around Waterstones for nearly half an hour before outstaying our welcome. Apparently, the staff weren't fans of Dougie knocking books off the shelves. Admittedly, that was my doing, channelling my power to send them tumbling whenever my pal walked by.

Have I not mentioned the power? Oh yeah, it isn't all bad.

There were a few little tricks I was learning, such as 'the push', where I could focus my ghostly energies into an act of force, causing effect in the living world. This had at first been triggered by emotions – fear, hate, love, all the rich stuff – but lately I'd been learning to channel it at will. It helped having a mentor – and we'll come to him later. Having been kicked out of the bookshop, we enjoyed the parkour boys pulling tricks in the Town Hall gardens before the police moved them on. We went gloom-spotting, watching the pocket-punks and mini-goths mope outside the alternative lifestyle boutique. With the leather, metal and tattoo paraphernalia on show in the window; 'boutique' was the last word I'd have used to describe that particular shop.

We even managed to bang on the window of Games Workshop before the manager gave chase. I know, what hell-raisers! That's right, even roleplaying gamers have their nemeses, and for us it was the thirty-something guy who ran that place. The world of fantasy gaming was as diverse and feudal as any other; tabletop-troopers and dungeon-dwellers just don't mix. Even we could be bigoted and close-minded. The tabletoppers no doubt also suffered bullying because their hobby was deemed nerdy or whatever label the brainless wanted to stick it with. We should have been brothers-in-arms, standing shoulder to shoulder in the name of geek liberation, not bickering with each other like dingbats.

We had taken the bus into town, the bus stop not being haunted like the train station. The Lamplighter's ghost cast a long shadow over those platforms, and Dougie was in no hurry to return there. Having enjoyed our morning's mischief and merriment, my mates had retired to the local burger joint to fill their faces. This consisted of nugget-shaped bites and buns packed with hosed-off cow-lips and bum-holes. I'd never been a fan of fast-food joints in life, and watching that pair scoff it down made it no more appealing in death. Food devoured and milkshakes in hand, the three of us exited the restaurant, in search of our final port of call for the day: the computer game store.

'Listen to this, too good to miss,' said Andy, heralding the arrival of a belch that made his teeth rattle. This would ordinarily have been resident clown Stu Singer's job, but in his absence, Andy had manfully stepped into the breach. A trio of girls walked past the other way, disgusted.

'It's a wonder you haven't found a girlfriend yet,' said Dougie. 'Truly it is.'

'I'm waiting for the right one to come along. It's not easy being this desirable.'

'Yeah, you're beating them off with a stick.'

Andy had never really had a girlfriend before. He snogged a girl at his thirteenth birthday party, but rumour had it that was his cousin (second removed as he'd once remarked in his defence). It would take quite the lady to distract him from his true love: roleplaying. Andy was married to his hobby. He had a clutch of new rulebooks and modules in his carrier bag, and was itching to rip into them.

'Hello girls.'

All three of us turned, our stomachs churning when we discovered Vinnie Savage and his henchmen were following us. Vinnie once dated Lucy Carpenter, Dougie's girlfriend, and he and my friend had come to blows not long after I'd died. It had been during Danger Night when the fair came to town, and Savage had received a punch to his guts – possibly his undercarriage. We were hazy about where the blow had landed. Dougie and he had disliked one another long before Lucy had entered the equation, Vinnie being a stone-cold bully of the lowest order. This was the first time Dougie had encountered him for a great many months.

'Vinnie,' said Dougie, his voice a strangled croak. It was worth remembering that, when the fabled fairground fight had taken place, it had actually been *me* who had punched Savage. It was my ghostly fist that had propelled him off his feet and into the mud, one of the first times I'd truly used the push to any effect. Dougie had taken the plaudits from everyone at school, but the punch hadn't been his.

'Scrote,' said Vinnie, ushering my friends back into the boarded doorway of a closed-down shop.

'Touché,' said I, before turning to Dougie. 'Any time you want to leg it, I'd suggest you start running.'

'I know,' said Dougie under his breath.

'What's that, Hancock?' said Savage, taking a step closer. 'Talking to yourself? I'd heard you were tapped in the head. Seems the rumour's true.'

Andy shifted anxiously beside Dougie, face drained of colour, eyes flitting for an escape route. Savage looked Andy up and down.

'This your girlfriend then, Hancock?'

Chuckles from the thugs at his back.

'No, she's at home.' The words were out of Dougie's mouth before he could help it.

'Way to wave the red flag at the bull,' I said as Savage's face contorted into an ugly snarl.

'You're still seeing my girlfriend, then?'

Dougie swallowed hard. Now he was up to his neck in it. 'She stopped being your girlfriend ages ago, Vinnie, before she started seeing me.'

Andy slurped nervously on his milkshake, drawing Vinnie's attention. The bully reached forward and took hold of the cup.

'That's mine,' said Andy, nervously, the straw pinging from his lips.

'And now it's mine,' said Vinnie, his voice a menacing whisper as he pulled the straw out and flicked a glob of milkshake at Andy. It hit him square on the forehead. 'See how that works?' He towered over Andy, making sudden aggressive movements with his head like some demented cockerel. He was intimidating our friend, who looked Dougie's way fearfully.

'Tell him not to fret,' I said. 'It's not like he's going to do anything here.'

Dougie echoed my comment. 'Don't worry, Andy. He won't do anything. Not in broad daylight.'

'No?' said Savage. 'You and me have unfinished business, Hancock. I don't know what you did on Danger Night, but it wasn't a fair fight. A sucker-punch to the guts is—'

'I thought it were your knackers, Vin,' said one of his sidekicks.

Savage glared, silencing him, before continuing. 'Hitting me unawares. That was a coward's trick. How's about we go for round two, now?'

Dougie was looking for a way out, past the three idiots, but my eyes were locked on Savage. The stolen milkshake juddered in his hand, white knuckles threatening to crush the cup in his grip, his face alive with twitches and tics. I'd seen him do it before, beating up kids in the schoolyard, building himself up to throw the first punch. The adrenaline was coursing through him now, sub-normal brain sending messages to his free hand: *make fist.* Dougie was still busy seeking an escape route. I found one for him.

'*Now*, Dougie!'

I shoved Savage hard in the chest, a powerful push that propelled him into his two cohorts. The gap was there and Dougie and Andy bolted for it. They were off up the road, fear adding fire to their stride as they weaved through the high street crowd. As I was pulled along after him, I could feel the sick nausea washing over Dougie and into me, the terror that they would catch him and what they might do. Andy peeled away, ducking into a coffee shop, while Dougie ran on, glancing back all the while. Savage was closing, charging through the sea of shoppers like a bloodhound. Dougie was so busy looking back that he didn't see the curly-haired man step in front of him, exiting the bank.

My friend crashed into him, causing the fellow to spin. The two were engaged with one another briefly, a mess of limbs as my pal tried to disentangle himself. Wallet, keys and loose change tumbled from Dougie's pocket, coins scattering the pavement as they danced. The man was rangy, wearing a smart black suit and pointy shoes. A businessman, no doubt, popping in to see his bank manager at lunch. Now accosted by a frantic teenager.

Dougie tore free and dashed out of the daylight into the dead-end alley beside the bank, slipping under the fire escape gantry and hiding in the shadows. I was by his side, poking my head back round the corner as my mate squealed for air.

'I feel sick,' said Dougie.

He wasn't alone. The push had exhausted me, the connection with the living world sapping me of my ghostly energies.

'Hush,' I said, stepping out to check the coast was clear. It wasn't. 'Crap.'

Dougie's frantic gasps were stifled instantly, but it was hopeless. Savage's hulking shadow approached down the alley. He must have seen Dougie dive into the little lane.

'Little pig . . . little pig . . .' chuckled the bully, also out of breath.

There was nowhere for Dougie to hide. He stepped out from beneath the fire escape, reluctantly accepting what was to come. I would have done anything to help him, but I was a spent force. I too felt sick; at that moment I wondered if ecto-plasm might actually be ghost-barf. I suspected I was about to find out.

'You're the big bad wolf, are you, lad?'

All three of us stopped. We looked to the head of the alley-way. It was the man with the mop of dark curly hair my mate had just crashed into. He was strolling towards us, dusting down that fine black suit. He picked a fleck of lint off his cuff and flicked it on to the breeze. I don't believe for a moment there was an actual piece of fluff there; he did this for effect, a show of cool, calm composure. He was gangly, wiry, a touch of the Cumberbatch in his ice-cold eyes as he glared at Savage.

'Cat got your tongue, Mr Wolf?' The man's accent was thick Liverpudlian. It sounded guttural to my provincial ears; aggressive. I knew instantly he was dangerous. With the sharp black suit and pointy black boots, he looked like a gangster. Or a Beatle. I was undecided.

Savage smacked his lips. 'It's between me and him.' He gestured at Dougie with a sloshing wave of the milkshake. The man's hand darted out and seized the drink from Savage.

'And now it's between you and me.'

'Who *is* he?' I asked Dougie. My friend didn't answer. He stood transfixed, a statue as the tables were turned.

The Scouser took a slurp on the milkshake, his face contorting as he copped the taste.

'Blueberry? That's mingin'!' He popped the lid off the cup and tossed it aside, slowly moving the drink over Savage's head. The bully could have run at any point in time, but he also remained frozen fearfully in place. The man tipped the cup and the freezing contents slopped out on to Savage's head, pouring over his face, into his ear, down his T-shirt, all over.

I heard our favourite bully cry at that moment. It didn't make me feel happy. I felt sorry for him. God knows why. You reap what you sow, that's the saying, isn't it?

'Run along home, Mr Wolf,' said the man as Savage loped off down the alley, sobbing as he went.

'Thanks,' whispered Dougie, still in shock. He began to edge around the man who remained where he stood, grinning all the while. The smile made me shudder. His teeth were bright, brilliant white. I was instantly transported back to my childhood, sat on the sofa, hiding in my old man's armpit as *JAWS* played on the telly.

'You dropped these,' said the man, his hand jingling with change as he extended his curled fist to Dougie. My mate opened his palm as the man emptied the wallet, keys and cash into it. In addition there was a crumpled twenty-pound note. For a fleeting second, he looked my way, past Dougie. Did he sense I was there? Could he see me? Or was my mind playing tricks? The man then set off back to the head of the alley.

'Um, the note isn't mine,' Dougie called after him.

'It is now,' said the man, as he stepped back into the sunlight. 'Tell your dad Mr Bradbury says hello.'

Then he was gone, carried away by the crowd.

'Who's Bradbury?' I asked Dougie.

My friend blinked and gulped.

'That's his boss, Will,' he said. 'Bradbury's his boss.'

TWO

Mums and Dads

The bicycle I'd received for my fifteenth birthday had been my favourite gift ever. It was all the more galling to see it now, completely bent out of shape, suspended from the shed wall by a couple of rusty nails. This was the bike that I rode religiously every day. The bike I was riding the night I was killed.

As presents went, it was undoubtedly the best. There had been stiff competition, of course, in particular the LEGO Death Star from my eleventh birthday. That was spectacular. Constructing a fully operational battle station with Dad's help had been a magical experience, that magic only shattered when I discovered he'd used superglue to construct his half of it. Dad never really did understand the appeal and versatility of the plastic bricks, bless him, much less the irreversible bonding power of industrial-strength adhesive.

Like the Death Star after Dad's bright idea, the bike was a ruin. The electric blue paint was peeling in places where the metal frame had twisted and buckled, the steel showing beneath. The front wheel was almost bent in two, while the rubber grips on the handlebars were still torn up from where they'd scraped along the tarmac. The fact that my parents had kept the bike meant an awful lot to me: almost every other sign that I'd lived there had been obliterated. My bedroom was now a home gym, most of my belongings donated to the local kids' hospice. That said, I'm sure Mum had a box of personal stuff stashed away in the loft. That's if Dad's model train set hadn't swamped it entirely by now. We never got to play with it as kids, but our mates' dads could often be found up there. As big boys' toys went, my father's choo-choos were da bomb.

I could hear Dougie talking to my old man in the garden, beyond the shed walls. I couldn't help but smile. Very kindly, he had agreed to pay my parents a visit on our way home from town, for the first time in many months. It gave me the opportunity to have a mooch around my old home, reminisce about my childhood and see what my folks had been up to. Poor old Dougie was presently locked into history's most boring conversation. He really was the best friend a lad could ask for. It was small talk of the smallest variety, as any chat with your mate's dad would be. It's hard to find common ground when one of you is a fifteen-year-old roleplaying game fanatic and the other is a forty-four-year-old postmaster whose only interests are steam trains and gardening. I heard Dad grunt as he dug up the vegetable patch, Dougie pursuing a futile choice of topic.

'So the mail goes from the post office straight to where it's addressed?'

'No.' An exasperated sigh.

'Really?' Dougie's voice was incredulous. Worst. Actor. Ever. 'I always imagined that's what happened.'

'No, it goes to the sorting office first,' said Dad, as he turned over the soil with his fork.

'And that's where the postmen sort it?'

Another grunt from Dad. 'Clue's kind of in the name, Dougie.'

'Yeah.' Awkward chuckles. 'Fascinating.'

'Sheila,' Dad called, clearly wanting to escape the exhausting chat, 'how are you getting on with that cordial? A man could die of thirst!'

I brought my attention back to the busted mountain bike. My smile faded. I had been cycling to Dougie's house that night, keen to gloat with the news that I'd stolen a kiss from Lucy Carpenter, the girl I'd fancied from afar throughout high school. I never saw the car that hit me. It came from behind, out of nowhere, the bike and I crumpling with the impact. The next thing I recalled was waking up at the General

Hospital. Only I wasn't waking up in a physical sense. Seeing my dead body lying there on a trolley in A&E had been a big fat clue that I'd shuffled off my mortal coil. Since then, I'd been learning how to control my powers, as well as coming to terms with being a ghost.

'Here you go, Geoff!' Mum called. I heard ice cubes tinkling in the cordial as she approached. Was there ever a nicer sound on a hot summer day? We were in the middle of a heatwave, not that I'd have known. I was cursed to wear the clothes I'd died in: winter coat and Doctor Who scarf (knitted by Mum) trailing down to my feet.

I stepped through the shed walls, out into brilliant sunlight. Dougie caught my eye instantly, sandwiched as he was between my folks as the tall glasses of juice were handed out. He took one gratefully.

'A lovely refreshing drink for you hardworking chaps,' said Mum, happy to be fussing them.

'If talking incessantly counts as hard work then Douglas must be parched,' said Dad, a wink breaking the barb of his comment.

'So how are you doing, young man?' asked my mum, ruffling Dougie's hair as he supped at his juice. 'It's been too long since we've seen you, Douglas. What's happening?'

It was never going to be easy for my mate to return here. It was no secret how close he and I had been in life. He was as dear to me as my own family and, for many years, Mum treated him as an extended part of our little clan. I often joked that he was the brother I'd never had – this had often just been to get a rise out of my actual brother, Ben, who was a couple of years my senior. This often led to a dead arm, but was always worth it.

'I'm good, thanks, Mrs Underwood. It's been a busy year at school.'

'How's that going?'

'Well, thanks. As in all subjects except for the D in Art.'

'Ooh, that's great news,' said Mum, patting Dad's shoulder and causing him to spill his cordial. 'Isn't that great news, Geoff?'

Another grunt from Dad, part acknowledgement, part irritation. Of course, the upturn in Dougie's grades hadn't been on account of his hard graft. Academically, it had proved beneficial for him to have me hovering over his shoulder like some ghostly Google app. I'd always worked hard at school and, team that we were, I passed on what I knew to him. Alas, even I couldn't help him with Art. There were preschoolers with better fine motor skills and mark-making ability.

'And how's your dad?' said Mum. Dougie flinched, imperceptible to my folks but I saw it. 'I haven't seen George in forever.'

'He's really well,' Dougie lied. 'Busy with work.' Since we'd bumped into Mr Bradbury in town, a cloud had gathered over my friend's head. It was clear he wanted to speak to his dad about the man.

'Is he still driving?'

Dougie polished off the drink, eyes fixed on me.

'Yes, mate,' I said to him with a nod. 'We can go. I'm done.'

Dougie wiped his arm across his mouth, handing the glass back to Mum and completely dodging her last question. 'Thanks for the drink, Mrs Underwood. Appreciate it.'

'Don't be a stranger, Douglas,' she said, giving him a big hug. 'Will may be gone, but that doesn't change how we feel about you. Isn't that right, Geoff?'

Dad smiled and reluctantly nodded. To be fair, he was the same with me when I was alive. It had always been tricky coaxing a conversation from him. That wasn't to say he didn't love me, and I don't doubt for a minute he was still fond of Dougie.

'It's been lovely to see you, Douglas,' said Mum as she escorted Dougie up the garden and down the path beside the house. 'Do pass our best wishes to your dad.'

'I shall, Mrs Underwood,' he said as she opened the gate. I leaned into Mum, kissing her lightly on the cheek. Whether I consciously used the push or not, I can't say, but she brushed her fingertips across her face.

Dougie set off down the street, saluting her as we went,

whispering to me all the while. She continued waving, as was her way, at least until Dougie was out of sight. 'You took your merry time in there.'

I waved to Mum too. Silly, as she couldn't see me, but old habits die hard. 'It's nice to go back and see they're doing so well. They kept the bike, you know?'

'Good on 'em. It's the least they can do since they turned your box room into a multi-gym. I love them and everything, but I'm glad to be out of there.'

'Don't worry, I'm not planning on dragging you back every week.'

'Twice a year is more than enough. Listening to your dad drone on is torturous. The United Nations should investigate him.'

'Seemed to me it was you doing all the talking!'

'Were you listening to a different conversation to me? Did you *hear* him bang on about the post office? Watching paint dry is more thrilling.'

We walked on to Dougie's house in fine spirits, laughing and joshing, but as we passed the graveyard and turned down his street, there was a noticeable deceleration in his pace. His strut transformed into a shambling trudge, his mood darkening, that familiar feeling leaking out of him and into me. Our connection never failed, each of us sensing the other's emotions, no secrets to hide. I sensed his trepidation as we approached his home, pausing momentarily outside the empty drive. We could hear the television's din within, its volume woefully high. What the neighbours thought of Mr Hancock I dreaded to think.

'He's in then,' I said.

'He's always in,' said Dougie, walking up to the front door and entering the house. 'I'm home, Dad,' he called over the noise, stopping by the glass-panelled door into the lounge.

'Hang on, son,' came the voice from within, rough and weary. We both heard the clinking of glass as his old man quickly tried to hide whatever bottles he'd been drowning in. Drinking in the day came as no surprise to us. We could see him moving through the mottled glass, reaching around the side of his armchair. Dougie rolled his eyes, pushing the door open, fed up of the pantomime.

Mr Hancock smiled from his seat, though his eyes told a different tale. They were bloodshot and watery, his face unshaven, and he'd been wearing those clothes since the previous week. I walked past, invisible to Dougie's dad, catching the empty brown and green bottles that had been stashed behind the armchair. The floor was littered with unopened bills and letters, the living room a pigsty.

'You having a bite to eat, son?' he asked, half-heartedly threatening to rise from his seat.

'I ate with Andy in town, thanks.' This was sadly typical of his father to be unaware of his movements, including where he got his last meal. 'You want anything? A cup of tea? Food?'

'I'm alright, Douglas,' said Mr Hancock, sniffing his nose and scratching his scrawny stomach. 'I'm not really hungry at the mo. May get something later.'

'Later?' I said. 'You *know* he hasn't eaten today, Dougie.'

'Let me make you some cheese on toast, Dad,' said my mate, clearly concerned for his father's welfare. 'It's not a problem.'

There had been a steady decline in Mr Hancock's well-being over the last year. It was heart-breaking to see. My earliest memories of him, when we were little, was of a cheery chap who would do anything for his son. Somehow, he'd begun to full apart recently. Miserable in his job, he'd all but jacked in driving for Mr Bradbury as far as we could tell, drinking away his sorrows at home. The pills he took to help him sleep were a great cause for concern, Dougie felt, and understandably so, in light of the booze. Mr Hancock never went out, never socialised, never invited his friends to call by. The man had become a recluse.

'No, son, really,' said Mr Hancock. 'I'm fine. Where've you been, then?'

'I already said, Dad. To town with Andy.' Irritation in his voice.

'Steady, mate,' I said, my voice a whisper even though his father couldn't hear me.

'Right, yes, so you did. You need to get out and meet girls, Douglas. That's what you need to do.'

Dougie looked at me. I'd witnessed this exact conversation many times in recent months. Mr Hancock had been told time and time again that Dougie was seeing Lucy, but it was pointless discussing it when he'd been drinking. It went in through one ear and out the other. My friend just shrugged, shaking his head. As for Dougie's girlfriend, that's something else I'd forgotten to mention. That girl who I'd loved from afar right through school, the one I'd stolen a kiss from the night I'd died? Lucy Carpenter. That's right. My best mate was now seeing her. I know. Some guys have all the luck.

'See you later, Dad,' said Dougie, slouching out of the room and down the hall. I watched him trudge upstairs, head bowed.

'Now probably not the best time to ask him about Bradbury?' I said.

'Maybe wait until he's sober,' he replied, 'whenever that might be.'

There was little I could say. I followed.

THREE

Past and Present

'Get outta town, Sparky! Best gangster movie? *Angels With Dirty Faces,* every day of the week!'

'Have a word with yourself, Yank,' said Dougie, dismissing our friend with a wave of the hand. '*The Godfather* is the best.'

'Jimmy Cagney!'

'Al Pacino!'

'Jim-mee Cag-nee!'

'Al Pa-chee-no!'

This was how conversations often went between Dougie and the Major, inevitably descending into a slanging match. It could have been a number of things that brought them to loggerheads. Perhaps it was the age difference. Maybe it was the cultural chasm, with the Major being American. More than likely, the biggest difference was: one was alive, the other a ghost. As always, I was torn, unable and unwilling to take sides. I grinned as a couple of nurses walked by across the hospital lawn, looking our way with concern.

'It's no good talkin' to you, Sparky,' said the Major. 'You get too emotional, shouting and making a scene.'

'You're shouting too!' said Dougie, defensively.

'Ah, yes,' grinned the airman's ghost. 'But they can't see me, can they? You're the crazy son-of-a-gun sat on the grass yelling at himself. Making me the winner.'

Dougie grumbled as I chuckled. 'Whatever. You're the loser as you've never seen *The Godfather*.'

'And probably never will,' sighed the Major. 'The drawback of haunting a hospital and not a movie theatre.'

We had first encountered the phantom American last autumn, when our friend Stu Singer had ended up in hospital after a fall from the Upper School building. I say 'fall': he was pushed, by our headmaster, who it transpired was a sadistic, murdering nutcase. That was all in the past now, Stu well on the road to recovery, and Mr Goodman dead and gone. The girl who he'd killed had been haunting an old school house, and it was she who had first taught me how to control my powers. Phyllis had been her name, and she'd opened my eyes to the possibilities haunting offered up. She vanished when Goodman died, leaving Dougie and me to seek out the Major for further guidance. It transpired the Major was a pesky soul, Dougie often the target of his mischief.

'I'm just kidding with ya, Sparky,' said the airman, punching Dougie's shoulder with a ghostly fist. He'd taught me the same trick, much to my friend's annoyance.

'Quit it,' snapped Dougie. 'That is so not cool.'

'So what do you guys have planned? You got the whole summer ahead of you. What do kids do round here? You got a beach house to head to? Catch some surf and rays?'

'Beach house?' I laughed. 'Nearest beach is the Mersey. And catching rays? You'd more likely catch blood poisoning.'

'I keep forgetting your British summers are different to real ones,' said the Major.

The Major was coy, never telling us his real name, but he'd been haunting the General Hospital since the 1940s. Like me, he was stuck in the clothes he'd died in, and he hadn't got around to explaining the circumstances of his death either. Across the left breast of his uniform a string of multicoloured pips revealed his rank. He was actually a captain, but Dougie and I had never let details stand in the way of a good nickname. 'Major' had stuck. When not hidden by his US Air Force dress cap, his jet-black quiff was slicked back over his head, topping off his movie-star good looks. As officers went, he was fresh-faced to have been made a captain, but wars, deaths and field promotions will do that.

'So tell me,' said the Major. 'What brought my favourite double-act here today? I wasn't expecting you until the week-end.'

Dougie kindly visited the hospital each Saturday, allowing me the opportunity to spend time with the Major. Dougie would watch on while the American talked me through what he knew, passing on tips and sharing his thoughts. We discussed everything, from how I'd ended up a ghost, the other spirits we'd seen or encountered, and what might have stopped me from moving on. The Major's ideas were just that: ideas. Neither of us had received an instruction book when we had become ghosts, although with Dougie's help we were doing a fine job of writing one. My friend would take notes on what we discovered, compiling a *Rules of Ghosting* handbook in the process.

Dougie reached into the back pocket of his jeans and pulled out a crumpled sheet of newspaper. He unfolded it, straightening it out, before laying it out on the grass before us.

'Ah,' said the Major, the spring taken out of his step. 'Way to ruin a guy's day, Sparky.'

We all looked at the headline: *AIRBASE TO BE DEMOLISHED.* This was where the Major had been stationed during the Second World War, one of many Yanks who had briefly made my sleepy little town in the north-west of England their home.

'What does this mean for you?' I asked.

'I've no idea,' said the Major. 'We've spent so long talking about what's keeping *you* here, in the land of the living, that we've given little thought to my own predicament.'

'Maybe that's it,' said Dougie. 'Perhaps when the old base finally gets bulldozed you'll be on your way?'

'You're all heart, kid. There could be some truth in that. I left some memories there, for sure . . .'

He drifted off for a moment, his mood melancholic. This wasn't like the Major at all. He was usually wisecracking, playing pranks and generally goofballing. Dougie and I shared a look of concern. The Yank was often evasive when his past came up, but he'd never fallen silent before.

'Should we head over there?' I asked. 'Is there something you'd like us to retrieve? After all, I think that's why I'm still here, to help people out, whatever their mortal state.'

The Major snapped out of it, a grin back on his face in a flash. 'I thought it was your bromance with Sparky here that kept you spooking about?'

'For the umpteenth time,' Dougie sighed. 'It's *not* a bromance. We're mates, that's all.'

'Mates with a beautiful, special, supernatural bond, eh?' said the Major, grinning impishly. 'Yeah, I got you two down pat!'

'So that's a negatory on visiting the airbase?' said Dougie, not allowing him to wriggle off the hook as he'd done so many times before.

The Major stood and straightened his uniform. It was the strangest thing watching a ghostly man, glowing pale blue, dusting himself down.

'Don't sweat it, kid. I'm good. It's this place I'm bound to, right? The hospital's my home. There's nothing for me at the base any more.'

'But what do you *do* here?' asked Dougie. 'As far as I can tell you stand at the entrance like a sentry. Hardly seems productive. The Lamplighter, however, haunts the railway station. His job's pretty clear: he scares the crap out of anyone who gets close.'

I shivered at mention of the Lamplighter, the only other spirit we'd encountered. Dougie and I had found ourselves on the platform late one night. A crooked killer's spectre that oozed wickedness, the Lamplighter had left me fearful for my life. Quite a trick, considering I was already dead.

'The Lamplighter's an old-fashioned malevolent spirit, tied to the scene of his crimes,' said the Major. 'Springheeled Jack for a new generation.'

'Exactly. He has a job description,' said Dougie. 'Even Will seems to have a purpose. He haunts the heck out of me, follows me around like a loveless, lonely, lost, little puppy that's been kicked up the butt.'

'Cheers for that.'

'You're welcome.'

'You're tied to the hospital,' I said, picking up my pal's thread. 'But why? I haunt Dougie. The Lamplighter haunts the station. Why do you haunt the hospital?'

The Major scratched his chiselled jaw. His teeth shone white as he flashed his ladykiller smile.

'I'm here to help: the "meet and greet" for new arrivals.'

'You weren't here for me.'

'You caught us *all* on the hop, kid.'

'How long are you here for though?' I asked. 'It's already been seventy years!'

'I really don't know when I'm supposed to clock off. I guess I'll figure it out when it happens.' He snapped his heels together and saluted me. 'As ever, it's been an absolute pleasure.'

He turned to Dougie, salute dropping. 'And you. Go away and watch some films. Good ones, this time. Preferably featuring Jimmy Cagney.'

With that, the Major strutted back toward the A&E, shouting, '*You dirty rat!*' as he went.

'What a colossal arse,' said Dougie as we watched him go. 'You really like him, don't you?' He didn't answer, but I spied a smirk appear on Dougie's face too. He shrugged.

'Suppose he's OK. For a Yank.'

FOUR

M&Ms

Dungeons and Dragons, so often the last bastion of teen male imagination, was no longer a sacred realm. Back when I'd been a living, breathing, dice-rolling young man, roleplaying games had been a refuge for me and my mates. Donning our armour and pointy hats of wizardry, we could sally forth, tackling all manner of monstrous mayhem in our make-believe world. Banter was bawdy and bloody, censorship crushed underfoot, as we submerged ourselves in our characters, playing out their adventures. There was only one thing could really upset the apple cart, and it had happened since my passing. A girl had joined the party.

This wasn't just any girl, either. This was Bloody Mary. When Dougie and I were first coming to terms with my haunting, we had enlisted the help of our resident school goth.

Mary had been in her last year at Brooklands, cutting an intimidating figure as she puffed away on her cigs behind the bike shed. Dougie had invited her back to his house under the pretence of seeking supernatural advice. After all, she was supposedly a medium and had the afterlife on speed-dial. Kids said she was the real deal. Then again, kids say a lot of things. It hadn't gone well. Crossed wires led to Mary thinking Dougie had the hots for her. Chaos had followed.

'OK,' said Mary, picking up the die and blowing it in her cupped hands. 'Momma wants a critical hit . . .'

The die flew, bouncing across the table past a bowl of M&Ms as Dougie, Stu Singer and Dungeon Master Andy Vaughn watched on. The multi-faceted icosahedron skittered to a halt.

'Boom!' she shouted, high-fiving Stu. 'Twenty! How d'ya like them apples?' Another roll of an odd-shaped die and Andy was left calculating the damage she'd dealt to the goblin king.

'Right,' said the Dungeon Master. 'Your battleaxe takes the king's head clean off, his ugly mug flying across the cave and into the crowd of onlooking goblins. They shriek and stampede, their morale broken.'

Mary whooped again, planting a sloppy kiss on Stu. That's right; they were an item. Some things really didn't need to be witnessed by others. The local vicar's son and Mary smooching topped that list.

Dougie seized his moment as the other two were distracted in celebration. 'Andy, can I creep forward and try the king's treasure chest? Firstly, I'll check it for traps and then—'

'Whoa, whoa, Nosebleed,' said Mary, pulling away from Stu's embrace. 'What do you think you're doing? I killed the king. I get first dibs on treasure.'

'Oops,' I said. 'You've awoken the kraken.'

This was how it went. Mary was full-blooded in her approach to gaming, wanting to win at all costs, even if that was to the detriment of others participating. Her half-orc barbarian only helped her intimidate her fellow players. Specifically Dougie. Stu happily went along with all she did. It appeared he rather enjoyed being dominated by her, and he was terribly easily led. Dougie's poor little halfling thief, Filo Bigfoot, never stood a chance.

'Look,' he said. 'I'm the thief, you're the fighter. Knock lumps out of the bad guys, but step aside when there's a chest to open. That's my area of expertise. Unless you fancy disarming a trap if there's one in there?'

Dougie waited for a response from a glowering Mary but none was forthcoming. You could have cut the atmosphere with a knife. Since the 'misunderstanding' on his and Bloody Mary's one and only date last autumn, each would have happily never set eyes upon the other again. For Stu Singer to then start seeing her had really put the cat amongst the canaries. There were certainly less volatile, incendiary girls out there that Stu might have pursued, but beauty was in the eye of the beholder. It was tough to argue with love.

Dougie nodded and dipped his hand into the dice bag, retrieving his lucky twenty-sided die. 'I'm going to investigate the chest for traps.'

'Right,' said Andy, revelling in the building atmosphere. 'You stalk carefully across the chamber, the sound of screaming goblins disappearing into the tunnels at your back. Your bare, furry feet step lightly across the ground until you arrive at the chest. Crouching, you open your lockpick kit as Priest of Pelor, Father Ivor Biggun—'

Stu laughed, but Andy ignored him, continuing.

'—and the hulking barbarian, Red Mary, watch on . . .'

Dougie kissed the die, shaking it in his hand. He prepared to launch it. We all craned in, waiting with bated breath.

'So, you and Will go and see the Major today then?' blurted Stu. As mood-killers went, it was one of his best. I chuckled, Dougie ceased his die roll and Andy groaned.

'You do this *every* time, Stu,' sighed Andy. 'Can't you stay *in character* for just one session?'

'Pfft,' said Stu. 'Where's the drama? We all know what's coming. The chest will be trapped and he'll cark it in some way or another. Happens every time. I've lost count of the number of times my priest has had to raise Filo Bigfoot back from the dead.'

'You really are the worst holy man ever,' said Dougie.

'He has a point,' I said. 'You do make a lousy thief.'

'Shut up, you,' said Dougie, turning to where I hovered on his shoulder.

'See, even Will agrees. He does, doesn't he?' Stu laughed. 'So, did he tell you his name yet?'

Ghost I may have been, but my existence was no longer a secret. Dougie may have been the only living soul who could see me, but I'd proved to the others – including Bloody Mary – that I wasn't just the fevered ramblings of Dougie's addled mind. I may have been invisible, but they certainly knew I was there. And they were cool with that.

'As it happens, we did go to see him, but no sign of his name yet,' said Dougie, putting the die down for a moment as he grabbed a handful of the M&Ms. 'Told him they're demolishing the airbase. It seemed to throw him.'

'You think that's it?' asked Andy. 'The air base gets flattened and *poof*, he's out of here?'

'No idea. He thinks he's waiting for a sign. His connection's with the hospital.'

'We should do some digging,' said Andy. 'Find out who he is. A captain in the US Air Force who died while stationed over here?'

'Get looking, pal,' said Dougie. 'He's not spilling the beans any time soon.'

'Is he going to roll the dice or what?' asked Mary.

'It's *die*, singular,' said Dougie, smiling at this small grammatical victory.

'You want to meet my *fists*, plural, Nosebleed?'

Dougie brought his attention back to the twenty-sided gem die.

'Detect traps roll please, Dougie,' said Andy.

'Come on, mate,' I said. 'Break the habit of a lifetime. Show them how it's done. Don't muck it up.'

Dougie kissed his lucky die once more, praying to his own deity, perhaps some little-known God of Hapless Hobbit Thieves. The die flew, bouncing off the bowl of M&Ms before coming to a halt in the table centre. We all peered at the number. It was decidedly middling: ten. This was either a good or bad thing for Dougie. Stu sucked his teeth as Mary giggled, Andy referring to his script.

'You don't detect any traps, Filo, your eagle-eyes searching for a needle within the lock. Your pick slips into the mechanism and after a few deft jiggles and cranks, you hear it click. It's open!'

Dougie grinned at the other two.

'Sadly,' continued Andy, 'you hadn't noticed the pressure plate on the flag you were crouched upon. The paving stones give way around you, dropping you into a thirty-foot pit trap on to a dozen five-foot iron spikes. Saving throw versus death please.'

'Well, he opened the chest,' said Stu.

'Can we search through the treasure now?' asked Mary.

'Sod this,' said Dougie, standing and scooping up his die and character sheet. 'I've got better people I could be with.'

'Oh yeah, who?' asked Stu.

'Lucy Carpenter, for one,' said Dougie, storming for the door.

'Fair point,' said Andy.

Dougie strodc back, reaching between the two lovebirds to snatch up the bowl of tiny colourful chocolates from the middle of the table. He emptied them out into his jeans pocket.

'And I'm taking my blooming M&Ms with me, too!'

FIVE

Friends and Family

It was crisp, clear summer evening, the sky scattered with diamonds. A night for romance, without a doubt, which made my proximity to Dougie and Lucy Carpenter all the more uncomfortable. The sound of their lips smacking would curdle the hardiest of stomachs. If I'd been remotely corporeal then my breakfast would have been making a sudden and violent reappearance. I couldn't even slope off; Dougie and I were connected via our ghostly umbilical cord, destined to never be apart. This was the worst part, where my spectral scenario really felt like a curse. I groaned as they chuckled over some private joke outside her front gate.

'Give it a rest, you dirty pigeons,' I called. 'Just say goodnight and be done with it!'

Dougie shot me a dark look that Lucy missed. I'd got things

wrong with Lucy. She was still a good person, no doubt, but my feelings toward her had never been reciprocated. I was just her mate, good old Will Underwood. After the incident with the wicked headmaster and the local celebrity that had followed, Dougie had been momentarily thrust into the spotlight. Everybody wanted to be his friend, nobody more so than Lucy. The idea that he was haunted by me had faded in her mind, and Dougie didn't overegg that point. It wouldn't have helped the relationship, knowing that a ghost hung around your boyfriend like a bad smell.

'Put him down, Lucy,' I added. 'You don't know where he's been!'

They were whispering sweet nothings. More subdued laughter. The jingle of the charm bracelet Dougie had bought her to celebrate six months as boyfriend and girlfriend. A couple of more smooches and hugs. Then she was trotting up the garden path to her door. There was a movement in the lounge window as a tall, stern-faced man appeared: Mr Carpenter. He glowered at Dougie, who smiled back politely. Lucy waved to my pal, the door closed and he strutted back to me, the king of all he surveyed. His grin made the Cheshire Cat look like a manic depressive.

'You're done eating her face?' I asked, falling in alongside him.

'For this night, yep.'

'For this night?' I groaned. 'Does that mean you want to see her tomorrow as well?'

'That's what boyfriends and girlfriends do, Will; see each other. Sorry, mate, but I didn't write the rules. I didn't plan for any of this to happen, and I'm sorry you have to see it. But life goes on. I fancied her too, you know. Everyone fancies her.'

It was true, Lucy was an incredibly popular girl. Clever, pretty, game for a laugh and from a good family. Foolishly, I'd assumed that just because I was infatuated with her nobody else could be. Dougie had clearly been terribly fond of her. I'd imagine Andy Vaughn was, too. Stu Singer . . . well, Stu was a fan of pretty much anything that moved. He wasn't fussy, present choice of girlfriend proving the case in point.

'I need to find someone for you, pal. Get you a date with some groovy girlie ghostie. We should ask the Major if he knows of anyone.'

'He'd probably hook me up with the Lamplighter, just for the giggles.'

Five minutes later and we were turning down Dougie's street, heading to his house. Dougie was still bumping his gums about Lucy. Gloating was so unseemly.

'You know, there *will* be somebody out there, Will. We already know you're not alone. We need to keep looking.'

'I'm not looking for love, mate. I'm looking for answers, specifically about what I'm doing here.'

'Haunting me, as far as I can tell.'

'But what's my *purpose*? Why am I still here?'

'Unfinished business seems the best bet. Whatever that is. And then you get to move on and join the Big Man upstairs and his choir invisible.'

'Who said I wanted to move on? I'm just after some answers, is all. And besides, aren't you too? I thought you were going to have a word with your old man about Bradbury?'

Dougie rubbed his chin ruefully. 'Not sure where to begin on that front. It's his job, isn't it? And Dad hasn't worked for ages. What do I say to him?'

'Hi Dad, met your boss yesterday – he's a real creep, isn't he?' I replied. 'Something like that, maybe?'

'He *was* odd, wasn't he? I know he saved me from Vinnie Savage, but I never asked for his help. And the manner in which he did it really weirded me out.'

'I know what you mean,' I said. 'Savage is a horrible cretin, but that was hard to watch. I know he's a bully, but Bradbury made him look like a kitten. Which begs the big question . . .'

'Which is what exactly?' he asked as he opened the front door and entered his house. We could hear the television set, loud as ever.

'How does your dear old dad end up working for a man like Bradbury? And why isn't he working any more? Bradbury didn't seem nice, but better the devil you know and, as you say, a job's a job, eh? I wonder what the deal is.'

'Let's ask, eh?' whispered Dougie as he opened the glass-panelled door into the lounge. 'No time like the present.'

Mr Hancock almost jumped out of his armchair at the sudden appearance of Dougie in the doorway. He looked as dishevelled as ever, but his smile was still on show for his son.

'Hi, Douglas. Everything OK?'

'Yeah, thanks. I met Mr Bradbury the other day.'

The smile was gone.

'Who?'

'Mr Bradbury. Your boss.'

Mr Hancock's red rheumy eyes squinted. 'How do you know it was him? How did he meet you?'

'I ran into him by accident in town. Dropped my wallet and he caught me up to give it back. How come you don't work for him any more, Dad?'

'It won't have been Mr Bradbury,' said the weary man.

'He told me to tell you he said *hello*. How did he recognise me, Dad?'

'He didn't recognise you,' said Mr Hancock. 'Must've seen your library card in your wallet or something.'

'He knew me,' said Dougie.

'If you see him again, ignore him,' said his dad, rising from his armchair for the first time in forever. He sidled by, towards the kitchen.

'Ignore him? That's a bit rude, isn't it?'

'I don't want you talking to Mr Bradbury. Not ever.'

'Why?'

Dougie followed him, his father filling the old stove kettle at the sink. He popped it on to the hob and lit the flame beneath. Then back across the kitchen, taking a mug from the sink, rinsing it out before dropping a tea bag in. He was doing everything but answer his son's question.

'Dad, why shouldn't I speak to him? He's your boss, isn't he?'

Mr Hancock placed a palm to his head as if attacked by a migraine. He was irritated, the words spat out fast. 'Not any more, he isn't! Is this an interrogation? Just do as I say, Douglas!'

'You might wanna back off,' I said, stepping in front of Dougie. 'Have you ever seen him like this? He's properly lost his rag.'

Mr Hancock was famously mild-mannered and quietly spoken. I'd never known him to show his temper. Maudlin, yes; depressed, often; but never furious. Dougie, however, was having none of it. This had been building for a while.

'Since when did he stop being your boss, Dad? You used to have a job, remember? You used to get up, go out to work, come home with money. You didn't sit in that damned chair drinking yourself to death. Is our life really so bad?'

'You don't understand, you're just a child.'

'Rubbish,' said Dougie. 'I'm the only one acting like a grown-up. You're not even eating any more. If social services got a whiff of what's going on here, they'd take me off you . . .'

'Go away,' his father muttered, beneath his breath.

'I'll be gone away soon enough, Dad, once I hit sixteen. Don't worry, I'll be out of your hair.'

Dougie stormed into the living room, slamming the partition door as he went. At the limit of my spectral tether to him, I remained in the kitchen, watching his father in front of the sink. Was he crying? I was useless at times like this, unsure of how to react and comfort somebody. It was especially difficult when you were a ghost.

'Don't worry,' I said, my words unheard. 'He'll come round. You will too. You have to get out of this funk, for your and Dougie's sake. Have a shower, a shave, put on a clean shirt and a smile. Call Mr Bradbury and ask for your old job back.'

He looked up. Did he hear me? I waved my hands to no reaction. Stupid to think he could.

He sniffed back the tears and reached across the counter, picking up the telephone. He paused, clearly considering what he was about to do. Then his finger was punching a number into the handset. He glanced at the lounge door; still shut. Taking a deep breath he lifted the phone to his ear. I could hear it ringing a few times before it was answered.

'Mr Bradbury?'

Had he heard me? He'd only gone and rung the bloke, hadn't he? Was he asking for his old job back? As it happened, the conversation took a very different turn.

'You don't speak to him again,' whispered Mr Hancock. His eyes were wet as he stared at the lounge door. 'Leave my boy alone, you hear?'

He didn't sound confident, his voice lacking conviction. If he was trying to sound threatening, it wasn't working. I had to get closer, hear what was being said on the other end of the line. I knew eavesdropping was an awful thing, but it came with the territory when you were invisible. I drifted right up to Mr Hancock, picking up the thick accent that crackled through the earpiece.

'He's your double, you know? You must be proud.' No answer from Mr Hancock. He gulped as the voice continued. 'Listen, we haven't seen you for a while, which is a real shame. It'd be good to catch up, find out what you've been up to.'

'We don't need to do that.'

'Don't be like that!' Bradbury sounded hurt, or was at least pretending to. 'We could get together, have a coffee morning.'

'That won't be happening.'

'Come on, George. It'd be good to get out of the house, wouldn't it? Can't be healthy, stuck indoors like a hermit, old before your years? Bit of fresh air would do you good.'

'Thanks, but I'm fine,' said Mr Hancock. 'Don't bother trying to get in touch with me again. I don't work for you any more, Mr Bradbury.'

'Now hang on. You forget. You and I *know* things. We've been through and seen some stuff, haven't we, George?'

Dougie's dad remained silent, refusing to acknowledge Bradbury.

'Way I see it, you can help me out. I've got a job coming up, and you're the perfect fit.'

'No thanks.'

'I'm not asking. I'm telling.' Mr Hancock drained of colour as Bradbury continued. 'Remember, I know your little secret. You kept it. I know you didn't get rid. So you'll do as I say, *capiche*?' No reply. 'I'll be in touch soon, George. Stay by the phone.'

'I do this one job, Mr Bradbury, and then we're done. For good. No more. And you keep my boy out of this. There's no reason for him to know anything.'

'Sure,' chuckled the man on the end of the line. 'Whatever.'

The phone went dead. Mr Hancock placed it back into its docking, hand trembling all the while.

What was *that* all about? What had I just witnessed? What

was Dougie's dad involved in? The kettle whistled on the stove, screeching angrily, as Mr Hancock whispered four sorry words.

'Please forgive me, Douglas.'

SIX

Dances and Dogfights

As double dates went, this one was weird. Dougie and Lucy had accompanied Stu and Mary to the hospital, our friend returning to the General Hospital for one of his once-a-month check-ups. These were visits to a spinal unit specialist regarding the variety of metal plates they'd put in Stu after his fall from the school roof. He was more machine than man, now. At least that's what he told everybody. He'd spent the first three months in a wheelchair as he recovered, and it was a miracle he could now walk. With Stu and Mary with his consultant, Dougie and Lucy remained in the hospital gardens.

I kept my distance, as best I could. I hadn't told Dougie what I'd overheard the previous day. How do you bring something like that up? '*Hiya, pal. Your dad's got a stonking secret. Thought you should know.*' Their relationship was already in bits. News like this would push it over the edge. Besides which, I didn't know *what* that secret was. It was clearly a whopper, judging by the hold Bradbury had over Mr Hancock. What did the man from Liverpool have on my friend's father?

'Ah, young love,' said the Major. 'Is there anything more beautiful?'

'Pass me the sick bucket,' I grumbled as Dougie and Lucy wrestled with one another. We were on the opposite side of an enormous rose bush display, two pale blue apparitions sat on a bench of our own. There were others in the garden too, patients and visitors alike. Old folk sat in their dressing gowns with grandkids at their feet. Younger patients grabbing fresh air together. Others stood in the smokers' corner, puffing away, seeking out altogether more horrid air.

'You disapprove of the romancing,' he said. 'Why?'

'I just don't need to see it.'

'You got the hots for her too?' said the Major, clicking his fingers. 'That ol' chestnut! Tough break, kid.'

I was going to deny it, tell him some big fat lie to cover my bum, but it was no good. The look on my face told him everything.

'It's just ... I always thought she and I would end up together. She was the last person who saw me alive the night I died. We'd just shared a kiss. Our whole lives lay ahead, who knew where they would lead?'

The Major raised an eyebrow. 'OK, for starters, you're fifteen years old, kid. Less of the *whole life* talk. It was probably just a kiss. You'd have got another, somewhere else, from another gal who rocked your world. There are plenty of fish in the sea.'

'But I never got to *see* where it was heading,' I said, shifting as I spied them snogging. 'She meant the world to me, Major.'

'You were infatuated, Will. She may not have felt the same way. Perhaps this was a blessing.'

'Me being dead? A blessing?'

'You know what I mean. It probably wouldn't have worked out.'

'What would you know? What makes you the world's greatest knowledge on love?'

'I know a thing or two,' said the airman ruefully.

'So you say, but why should I believe you? You tell us nothing about who you are, dodging that bullet every time. Secrets? You're just like Dougie's dad.'

'Sparky's dad's keeping something from him?'

'Yes, I overheard Mr Hancock on the phone, speaking to this bloke, Bradbury. He knows something that sounded really dodgy, and Dougie's old man's keeping that from him. How do I tell him something like that? Their relationship's already a mess. It's hopeless.'

'You gotta be straight with Sparky. Tell him what you know.'

'I can't, it'll kill him.'

'Not telling him will cause more harm. He's your best friend, Will. You gotta do right by him.'

'And why should I take your advice anyway? You're a closed book.'

The Major sat in silence as I stewed on his words. He removed his hat, smoothing a pale blue hand over the phantom material, running a finger along its visor. It wasn't my place to press him. If he wanted to open up, he would. It was a cheap trick to hit him with a comment like that.

'I'm Captain Chip Flowers and I was born in Columbus, Ohio, 1910.'

A cheap trick that worked! The airman's ghost continued.

'I was thirty-three years old when I died. Yeah, young. In wartime, all kinds of promotional opportunities pop up when you least expect 'em, usually preceded by a bullet.'

His demeanour shifted to one of introspection as he reminisced. He was being open for the first time, and I feared if I said something it'd be gone, snuffed out.

'I'd been stationed here for twelve months, but it was long enough. We had an incredible time, me and the boys. The girls of your fair town certainly made us Yanks feel welcome. The boys – less so. If we weren't chasing the ladies, promising them chocolate and nylons, we were being chased by mobs of local guys, angry that we were stealing their gals. In between that excitement, we trained hard at the base, preparing for war. Our lives consisted of drills, dances and dogfights. It was glorious.'

He stopped and smiled.

'There was one girl. Ruby. I didn't have a string of girlfriends like some of the boys. I'd courted in my youth back home, but nothing serious. That's why I tell you not to dwell on what might've been. But Ruby? Beautiful creature, mysterious too. Can you believe she *never* told me her surname? The minx! I thought I'd come to England to get ready for the fight, not fall in love. My best friend fell for her too, Josh Hershey, spelled like the chocolate bars. He asked her to marry him and she just laughed; thought the poor sap was joking! She only had eyes for me, though – kinda made things awkward for me and Josh for a while there.'

He nudged me in the ribs with his elbow.

'I never got to tell her how much she meant to me. I was going to propose. I had that stolen from me. She never knew.'

We sat in silence. It made all my dramas seem insignificant, certainly regarding Lucy, anyway. The Major – or Chip, to use his real name – had made me see things a little clearer. The jealousy goggles were off, never to be replaced.

'When I tell you to be straight with your mate, I mean it, Will,' he said, his voice sincere. 'Never have regrets about what could've been. Seize the day. Don't keep secrets from those you love.'

'Thanks, Chip,' I said, the man grinning as I used his name for the first time. 'Chip. Kind of sounds weird after calling you Major for so long.'

'It can be our little secret,' he said with a wink, replacing his peaked dress cap and straightening it upon his head.

'I thought you said no more secrets?'

'Dang, I *did*, didn't I? You're good, Will Underwood. You're very good.' He stood and stretched as if stiff and sore, completely pointless for a ghost. 'Lordy, but you get to my age and things start to ache. Come on, let's go and break my name to Sparky.'

'He's with Lucy,' I pointed out. 'Might wig him out if we start talking to him mid-smooch.'

'Fair point,' he said. He clapped his hands, signalling that he'd arrived upon a remarkable idea.

'What is it?' I asked, keen to hear his plan.

'Let's go pull faces at him from over her shoulder.'

And like that we were off, dashing through the rose garden to gurn at our buddy. It really was the least a friend could do.

SEVEN

Telltales and Truths

The rest of that day flew by. My chat with the Major (we decided to stick with our favourite moniker) had given me a fresh perspective. I hoped they got their shot at happiness that others, such as the Major and I, would never get. Especially the Major. His story was sad beyond words. He *had* found love, only for it to be snatched away. There was always somebody worse off than you. I was able to tag along with Dougie and Lucy, no longer feeling like a gooseberry. And if they happened to kiss, so be it. There were worse things to witness in life, apparently.

That evening, Dougie was at home. He wasn't seeing Lucy. I know; whodathunkit? Perhaps he was suffering from snog exhaustion, his lips chapped from so much action. Instead of reclining in the divine Miss Carpenter's embrace, he was lying prone on his bed, Xbox remote in hand as he battled his way through Skyrim. He made a surprisingly accomplished Battle-Mage. Better than a halfling thief, anyway.

We were a couple of days into the summer holidays and, bar our encounter with Vinnie Savage, we had many reasons to be cheerful. The business with Dougie's dad and Mr Bradbury, however, left a brooding cloud overhead. One that still needed broaching with my mate. But how?

'Shoot him in the eye!' I shouted as Dougie's character went head on with a dragon. It was my go-to phrase to shout at my mates whenever we played computer games. He could have been playing Minecraft and I'd still have yelled it. It was meant to irritate and put them off. It was working.

'Sod off!' he laughed, eyes wide with concentration, fingers feverishly working the controls. 'I kill this big lizard, I get the treasure!'

'Never. Gonna. Happen.'

A gout of fire erupted from the dragon's jaws, showering Dougie's Battle-Mage with liquid flames. He was too slow reaching for a healing potion. He stumbled and fell, ablaze. Quite dead.

'Ahem,' I said. 'Not saying I'm psychic or anything, but I think you need to update the *Rules of Ghosting* handbook.'

'Lucky shot,' said my mate, waiting for the game to reload.

'Yes. Being engulfed by a ball of fiery death was pure fluke. You had him on the back foot there, pal.'

As our laughter subsided, the *Coronation Street* theme drifted upstairs from the lounge, the volume set ridiculously loud as ever. It gave me a way in to the conversation I'd been dreading.

'Has he said any more about that business with Bradbury?'

'Nah,' said Dougie. 'Doubt he will now. Whatever bad blood there is, we'll never know.'

'You should dig a little deeper. There's something your dad's not telling us.'

Dougie stopped the game, hitting the pause button.

'You what?'

'Your dad's involved in something with Bradbury, something he hasn't told you about.'

'Hang about,' said Dougie, tossing the controller aside as he rolled over to face me. 'You have my full attention now, Will. Spill.'

I sighed. Judging by his less-than-friendly body language, Dougie wasn't going to enjoy hearing this.

'I overhead your dad on the phone last night. He was talking to Bradbury. Sounds like he has some kind of "big secret" he's been keeping from you. You should ask him about it.'

'You were eavesdropping?'

I shrugged. 'Comes with the territory. But I know what I heard.'

'You're aware you're basically calling my dad a liar?'

'No,' I said, trying to remain calm. This wasn't going at all well. 'I'm saying he's not telling you the whole truth.'

'I don't believe this.'

'I'm being straight with you here. I don't want to keep anything from you. You're my mate.'

'You're stirring is what you're doing,' said Dougie, angrily. 'Is this your way of getting your own back, turning me on my dad?'

'Hang about, Dougie. I'm *coming* to you with this, so you can do something about it. Your old man's involved in something – or was, in the past – and it's come back to bite his bum now.'

'So Dad's a criminal, that's what you're saying?'

'You're putting words in my mouth—'

'No, carry on. Tell me what you *really* think of him. He's a mess, isn't he? A gibbering, drunken, embarrassing mess. And your folks are just *so* perfect, aren't they?'

This was *very* bad. Things were spiralling rapidly out of control.

'Now wait a minute—'

'You can't stand the fact that Lucy's with me, can you? That's what this is all about. Wrap it up however you want, *mate*, but this boils down to good old-fashioned jealousy.'

'Sod off! I'm not jealous!'

'Yes you are! You've been like a kicked dog ever since we started seeing each other. Face like a wet weekend. I know you fancied her, but you're gone. I'm not. Should I ignore my feelings?'

'You?' I shouted, my own anger now getting the better of me. 'Feelings?'

'Damn right,' snarled Dougie. 'Feelings! That's why I've pandered to your every whim since you died, tolerated your creeping around like my flaming shadow every minute of the night and day. See, that's what mates do, Will. They make sacrifices. It's me that's taken you wherever you want, whenever you want.'

'Oh yeah?'

'Yeah. Popping round to your folks for awkward conversations after I haven't seen them for months. Trips to the hospital so you can spend time with your mate, the Major. I do all this for you, and do I grumble? You won't allow me a moment's happiness with Lucy.'

'This *isn't* about Lucy,' I said, regretting any previous moodiness. I'd turned a new leaf since my chat with the Major, but the epiphany had come too late. I was already damned by my actions.

'It's always about Lucy!'

'I'm trying to help you see the bigger picture, but you just won't listen, you idiot.'

'You patronising sod,' said Dougie, and took a swing.

Ordinarily, such a punch would have flown straight through me, sending him on to his bum. For whatever reason, probably the anger and raw emotion that had boiled up between us, the old rules didn't apply. His punch connected with *me*, his knuckles catching me flush on the chin. My head recoiled and I reeled back, through the air, through the bed, staggering through the wall and on to the landing. Dougie followed, appearing in the doorway to his bedroom.

'Stay away from me, Underwood.'

He slammed the door as I nursed my jaw.

'If only it were that easy.'

EIGHT

Dames and Names

The next three days saw my relationship with Dougie plummet to never-before-seen depths. We went from best of friends to the finest of enemies. For the first two days we said nothing to one another. I was the shadow we'd joked about, following him, impossible to shake. He spent time with Lucy – a *lot* of time. Perhaps he was trying to rub my nose in it, I couldn't say. He'd got me wrong in tremendous fashion, and I had no hope of persuading him otherwise. So I kept my back turned, tried to shut them out, ignored what was going on behind me. In his crueller moments, Dougie would occasionally mention me to her, recounting embarrassing stories from my extensive back catalogue. But he couldn't shake me. I was going nowhere. I was haunting him, for real.

Dougie was hurting, that much was clear. The words he'd

thrown at me during our row still rang in my ears, much of which was true. He *had* gone out of his way to help me. How had I repaid him? I'd been sulky over his relationship with Lucy. I felt bad about it, only realising my stupidity after my chat with the Major, but it all seemed so terribly late now. The cannon had fired, the horse had bolted, and I was covered in manure.

The third day saw Dougie catching up with Andy and Stu. Previously, whenever I'd anything to say to them, Dougie acted as a conduit. He was the mouthpiece, passing on my comments. Only now, sat in the public library, he wasn't being quite so helpful. As the three of them trawled through the local records, searching for the Major's old flame, Dougie didn't acknowledge me once. He actively ignored me. If the others asked me a question, he'd tell them I was exploring the library. It was hopeless; he'd cut me out. I was farting into a gale.

'*Captain* Chip Flowers? So he wasn't a major after all?' asked Stu, rifling through the DVD library beside the computer terminal.

'Try and keep up,' said Dougie.

My former best friend might have been ignoring me, but at least he'd returned to the topic at hand. The Major was a mate to both of us, and Dougie had never been one to shy away from a challenge. There was investigating to be done. He leaned on the back of Andy's chair, peering over his shoulder, our Dungeon Master working his magic on the keyboard. His fingers were a blur, searching through the Births, Deaths and Marriages website.

'Says here twelve men died when the base was bombed,' said Andy with a shiver. 'Maybe that's how the Major kicked it? Have to say, though, this is like searching for a needle in a haystack.'

'Chip's a nickname for Charles, right?' said Dougie.

'Right, but there's no point in looking for him. He's not the focal point of my search. There'll be nothing connecting him to any local woman. All I have to go on is Ruby, and there were forty of them alive in the town around that time.'

'She'd have been somewhere between fifteen and thirty-two years of age I reckon,' said Dougie. 'The Major said she was younger than him.'

'That brings the number down to twelve lovely ladies.'

'How many were married?' asked Stu. 'I mean, during the war years.'

'Before or during? There's quite a difference.'

'I dunno. Look for both.'

The fingers tapped away, Andy squinting through his glasses as he inspected the monitor.

'You think the Major's still here because of this Ruby lass then?' said Stu.

'Possibly,' said Dougie. 'The pattern seems to be great love or great trauma keeps ghosts here.'

'Or both together,' I added, but he didn't respond.

'Alright,' said Andy. 'Six were married before the war had begun and three more of them married during the war years.'

'What years were they married?' asked Dougie, thinking hard now, his brow knotted.

'Two in 1940 and one in '42. Is that important?'

'Yes. We can rule those three out also. The Major told Will that he was born in 1910 and died when he was thirty-three years old. So the Ruby he was in love with must have been single in 1943, by my reckoning.'

'Good work, Sherlock,' I said, hopeful for a reaction, but got zilch back. Dougie continued talking.

'So, we have three left. What happened to them?'

Andy shrugged. 'Two of them married after the war, the other remained a spinster until her death in 2001.'

'So,' said Stu, spinning the DVD rack, 'our mystery lady's one of those three?'

'Can we rule out the one who passed away?' asked Andy.

'Why?' asked the vicar's son.

'Well, if it *is* love that's keeping the Major here, then doesn't it make sense, with that Ruby having died, that he'd have joined her? Crossed over to the other side when she did?'

'We can't rule her out,' said Dougie. 'If it *was* her, and we can't be sure, then it doesn't necessarily hold true that with her passing the Major could move on. I don't think ghosting's as simple as that. He could be here until the next millennium, patrolling those hospital corridors.'

'She sounds dodgy to me,' said Stu, as I manoeuvred closer to Andy, beside Dougie. My old mate glowered at me briefly, disapproving of my proximity, but I ignored him.

'Dodgy?' asked Andy, leaving the three remaining ladies highlighted on the screen. 'Why's that?'

'Imagine, not telling someone your name? What was she hiding?'

'She may have been hiding nothing,' said Dougie. 'Just being flirtatious. Mysterious.'

'Perhaps she came from an important family,' said Andy. 'Could've been controversial if folk knew she was seeing a GI. After all, not everyone welcomed the Yanks.'

I was half listening to them as they discussed the various possibilities, but my attention was focused on the computer monitor, specifically the women's names.

Stu smiled smugly and shook his head. 'You two muppets aren't seeing the big picture. What if she was *married*? Have you not thought about that? Her bloke could've been overseas, fighting. Or he could've been the local butcher, who knows? What I'm saying is that the fact she never told him her surname casts a massive question mark over who it might be. We could be back to looking at twelve again.'

'Call off the search,' I said. 'I think I've found her.'

'You what?' said Dougie, his first words to me for three days. 'What makes you think it's her and not any of the others?'

I pointed a shimmering blue finger at one of the three we'd whittled it down to. Of those three, it was one of the women who had married after the war.

'Ruby Hershey,' I said. 'Like in the chocolate.'

'Eh?' said Dougie.

'Is that Will?' asked Andy.

'What's he saying?' said Stu.

It was the one piece of information I'd failed to pass on to Dougie after my heart-to-heart with the Major. I didn't think it had been important, hadn't figured upon it having a piece to play in the puzzle until it was there before my eyes.

'Hershey as in Josh Hershey,' I said, sighing as I recognised the tragic parallel. 'He was the Major's best mate, the guy who asked Ruby to marry him but she turned him down for Chip.'

I turned to Dougie, his face pale as he caught the irony too. When he spoke to our friends, his voice was fragile.

'She married the Major's best mate.'

'The Major's mate,' tutted Stu. 'Worst. Friend. Ever.'

NINE

Beggars and Blackmailers

I don't know whether it was my inspired catch on the whole Hershey thing that did it, but a distinct thaw in my relationship with Dougie followed. He no longer ignored me, answering questions in a fashion, either with nods, single-syllable words or reluctant grunts. So long as we stuck to the topic of ghostly mysteries, we were on safe ground, but anything regarding family or friends was strictly off limits. For me to bring up Lucy Carpenter or Mr Hancock would've been insane. We weren't best mates – I doubted we ever would be again – but we were talking, and that was something.

Dougie stood by the hob, the saucepan of beans bubbling, as he pasted butter over four slices of toast, two for each plate on the work surface.

'So we're calling in on the Major at some point in the next few days?' I asked optimistically.

'Mmm.'

'We need to tell him what we've discovered about Ruby.'

'Yup.'

'I was also wondering – and shoot me down if this sounds too stupid – could we revisit the railway station? Perhaps in daylight? Check out the theory that the Lamplighter's cursed to remain there and can't leave? It'd be good to know for sure.'

Dougie said nothing, taking the saucepan off the heat and carrying it over the plates of toast. He poured the gloop out on to the slices of steaming bread as I yammered on.

'See, I'm wondering if there's some way we can banish him? Exorcise him like Reverend Singer suggested that time? Stu says his dad knows people, right? Getting an evil spirit vanquished once and for all has to be a good thing. I'd call it a win for us if it worked.'

Dougie clattered the pan on to the hob. He turned to me, his face humourless.

'There *is* no "us" any more, Will. You were always the bright one, surely you can see this? We're stuck together, like it or lump it. We can move on, but I can't forgive and forget what you said.'

'Mate, we've both made mistakes, said some dumb things—'

'Stop calling me "mate", Will. We'll go and see the

Lamplighter, like you suggested.' He picked up the two plates, cutlery in his shirt pocket. He cocked his head and smiled. 'Who knows? If we *can* banish his ghost, perhaps that's the good deed that finally sends you on your way, eh?'

I didn't reply as he walked away. It seemed he took a touch too much pleasure from that last comment.

'You can but hope,' I whispered, before following him through to the lounge.

Mr Hancock was already hunched forward in his armchair, cutting a corner off a slice of bean-topped toast. He was putting it away, clearly hungry. I wondered when he'd last had a meal. The empty bottles were visible behind the chair, as were the pills he took, the bottle sitting on the cabinet beside him.

Dougie sat on the sofa, plate in lap, less enthusiastic with the feast before him. They ate in silence for a minute, Mr Hancock's gaze fixed upon his plate.

'When are you going back to work, Dad?'

Mr Hancock's knife screeched as it cut along the plate, causing me to jump. He smacked his lips, clearing his mouth of mashed-up beans and bread. He was in no hurry to answer, carefully considering a response.

'I'm not sure, son. Perhaps I'll pop along to the surgery tomorrow, see what the doctor can prescribe. These pills help me sleep, but I need something to wake me up, I reckon. Then maybe I'll be good to work.'

'You could always try drinking coffee instead of booze.'

There was no instant comeback from his father. He sawed at his second slice of toast, as if he hadn't heard Dougie.

'I'm sure I can get back into work, Douglas, just as soon as I clear my head.'

'Your head's been fogged for ages, Dad. The only way you're returning to work is by quitting drinking.'

'I know, son, really I do. I promise, I'll knock it on the head once I'm done with what's in the house.'

'You've promised me that before.'

'Well, I mean it this time.'

Dougie placed his plate on the floor, the food barely touched.

'Just because they're in the house, doesn't mean you *have* to drink them, Dad. You could pour them down the sink right now.' He rose from the sofa. 'I could help you. Come on—'

'Sit down, son. Maybe later, eh?'

Dougie shook his head. 'It's always later. Why won't you get out of that armchair? What's *really* stopping you from going back to work? Why do you no longer work for Bradbury? What happened?'

Mr Hancock slammed his cutlery down. 'I've told you already, we're not going to talk about Mr Bradbury.'

'You're wrong. That's exactly what we're doing.'

I could see tears in Dougie's eyes. I'd never seen him make

a stand against his father like this. He'd never had to. Mr Hancock had always been such an easy-going, mellow chap. It was only recently that he'd fallen apart, in the last few months. He was a mess of the man he'd once been, his own son now his nursemaid. If Dougie didn't cash the disability cheques and dip into the old man's bank account when needed, there'd be no food on the table. The situation was dire – and Dougie had reached breaking point.

'I know about the phone call, Dad.'

Ouch. He'd brought *that* up. And he'd said he hadn't believed me!

'What phone call?'

'Your one with Bradbury that you tried to hide from me.'

'How the hell—'

'Does it matter how I know? You're keeping something from me. What is it?'

I could see Mr Hancock was getting angry, his knuckles white as they gripped the plate in his lap. He hadn't been prepared for this line of questioning. Dougie had the scent and wasn't stepping down.

'Is Bradbury blackmailing you? What hold does he have over you? What did you do for him? Is he into something dodgy, or what?'

'Douglas, it's better if you don't—'

'But I *want* to know. I need to! Whatever's gone on affects us both, clearly. Why are you so dead set on not working for him. If it isn't something dodgy that's stopping you, then what is it?'

'You don't understand—'

'Then *help* me understand, Dad,' said Dougie, rushing to his father's chair to beg at his feet. 'I want to help you. But there can be no secrets. I need to know what's happened.'

'Stop it, son,' whispered Mr Hancock.

'We can do anything when we work together. I can see what it's doing to you. Let me—'

'I said, be *quiet*!'

Mr Hancock stood so suddenly that Dougie fell over. He smashed the plate into the fireplace, sending toast crusts and shards of porcelain across the hearth. His hands made fists at his sides. I did the same, stepping between father and son, channelling my energy. Should his old man do something stupid and out of character, I'd try and protect my friend.

Instead of striking Dougie, he grabbed a couple of bottles from beside his chair and left the room. We heard the key turn in the door that led from the kitchen into the garage. Mr Hancock slammed it behind him, locking himself away in there. Dougie wept where he lay as I stood stunned.

'Well,' I whispered. 'At least you got him out of his armchair, mate.'

There were no smiles. There was no laughter. It didn't look like there would ever be laughter again.

TEN

The Staff and the Shadows

I'd expected Dougie to head to Lucy's house after such a ruckus with his dad, but it didn't happen. Perhaps it was too late for a sudden appearance on her doorstep. Or she was out with her girlfriends. Maybe the last person he wanted to see when he was feeling so angry was Lucy. Whatever his reasons, we found ourselves heading somewhere altogether more thrilling. Ghost I may have been, but my heart still trembled with anticipation.

'It's not you, Dougie. It's Bradbury, like I said.'

'It must be awful being a smartarse.'

'Well, I don't like to bang on about these things, but I *was* right.'

'Yeah, buggerlugs,' he grumbled. 'Pays to be an eavesdropper, eh?'

The fight with Mr Hancock had brought the two of us closer again. The monosyllabic grunts had given way to actual conversation now, as Dougie let off steam. He didn't want to hear that I'd been right all along, of course, so I tried to go easy with the gloating. Tried. I may not have succeeded.

'This doesn't change what I said about Lucy, you know?' he said. 'You've been a royal pain in the butt when she's been around.'

'And I'm doing something about it, I promise.'

'Pie-crust promises. They break awfully easily.'

'So why here, tonight?' I wanted to get his mind away from the unhappiness at home and on to the bowel-shattering, gut-scrambling, squit-inducing horror that possibly awaited us.

'Seemed as good a time as any. There are a lot of questions about him that need answering. Maybe he'll be in a talkative mood!'

'Talkative?' I choked on the word. 'I thought we were visiting in the daytime though?'

'You're a ghost who's scared of ghosts now?'

'Of this one, deffo.'

'I can't see us finding him in daylight. The station's used during those hours. It's busy, full of people, unlike now. It'll be closed. Remember, it was Danger Night when we saw him.'

'How could I forget?'

Danger Night was the scam pulled by the fairground that

came to town once a year; one night in which all rides were half price because they hadn't been safety checked. Preposterous to anyone with a smidgeon of intelligence, but the neighbourhood kids got a buzz out of that frisson of peril, and even we managed to get swept away by it. As it happened, that night really *did* turn out to be dangerous. We had hidden on the railway platform from Vinnie Savage and his gang, only to discover something far scarier awaited us: the Lamplighter's ghost. I shuddered, recalling his awful apparition.

'So,' said Dougie, halting on the road at the top of the embankment. The footpath led down to the station. 'That's why we're here.'

He strolled down the incline and I followed. We left the safety of the streetlights behind us, the bridge's dark arch threatening to swallow the tracks below. I could sense Dougie's anxiety and no doubt he got a bucketload of mine. My stomach was in knots, nausea hitting me as we neared the platform. See, it had been *me* the Lamplighter had come for that night, not my mate. The Hancock lad wasn't the object of the ghost's hatred, its ire. It had a hankering for Underwood and nothing else would do.

Dougie came to the gate at the bottom of the footpath. He turned to me, arms folded.

'What?' I said.

'Off you trot.'

'Eh?'

'Get in there, go see if your pal's knocking about. Let's test the Major's theory that he's tied to the station and can't leave.'

'You're kidding, right?'

'I wouldn't kid about this, Will. I'm not going in there unless I really have to. At least on this side of the gate I'm clear for a quick getaway, should the need arise.'

'Should the *need* arise?'

'Aye, if things go pear-shaped. It's alright for you, you can slip through 'owt. Not so easy for me. I'd rather have a clear sprint if he doesn't fancy visitors.'

'Because he was *so* welcoming the last time we met him,' I said, phasing through the gate and on to the platform.

The station was empty, the ticket office locked up for the night, shutters down, door padlocked. I looked down the tracks in each direction. Eastbound toward town, the tracks disappeared through the bridge arch, the road running over the top of it. To the west, the rails shone in the moonlight, cutting through the natural woodland that crowded the train line. I walked along the platform, peering into every nook and cranny within the station house, searching for any sign of the Lamplighter. I looked up at the old gas lamps, rusting and redundant. I was waiting for them to spark into life, just as they had on Danger Night, but they remained dead and dull. I stared down the shimmering tracks, searching for movement and finding nothing. I turned back up the rails toward the bridge, squinting into the gloom. Two lights approached down the line, no doubt the last express on its way through the village to Liverpool. You never got stoppers at this time of night. I stepped away from the platform's edge as the lights neared, keeping my focus fixed upon the station.

My skin was suddenly crawling, cold dread creeping through me. It had been so long since I'd been aware of temperature I'd forgotten the sensation. My ethereal flesh rippled with impossible goosebumps as my attention was drawn back to the bridge's arch. Trainspotting 101: trains usually make a noise as they approach. The two glowing lights that blossomed in the blackness carried no such telltale soundtrack. His eyes burned with a terrible fire, white hot coals on an ebony field.

The Lamplighter stepped out of the darkness, peeling away from the stone archway and coalescing before me. His spindly legs carried him along the platform, long coat wrapped about his skeletal torso. He struck his staff against the floor and a flame burst into life at its head. One after another the old station lamps flared, balls of blue light rolling within them. I didn't need any further prompts.

I scrambled back the way I'd come, the hare having coaxed the hound into the hunt. Dougie screamed my name, pointing out the obvious all the while.

'Run, Will! He's here! He's coming! He's right behind you!'

'Cheers, mate,' I replied as I dashed towards him. 'You'll let me know if he grabs me?'

I passed straight through the locked gate and Dougie as the two of us toppled clear of the phantom. We fell on to the footpath, a jumble of limbs both solid and ghostly. We looked back as the Lamplighter halted at the station's threshold, his stovepipe hat adding another foot to his already towering frame. He turned his blackened skull one way and the other, up and down the long mesh fence. Craning his neck forward, dirty scarf trailing against the gate, the Lamplighter brought his lighting pole back before swinging it out, over the gate and towards where we crouched. We both gasped as it *whooshed* forward, a ghastly scythe looking to sever heads from stalks. The moment the staff passed over the gate and the station's border, it dissipated, leaving a trail of black smoke in its wake.

The Lamplighter hissed with disappointment. We sighed with relief.

'Come to taunt a hungry old man, have we, children?' His voice was the whisper of knives down our spines. 'It has been too long between meals, young ones. So cruel. Two feasts, one of flesh, one effluvial, and both beyond reach.'

His dark tongue flickered as he smacked his withered lips. They cracked with each movement, scorched skin splitting and falling in flakes.

'Well, he hasn't eaten us,' Dougie whispered. 'That's a start, eh?'

I cleared my throat. 'We've met before, Lamplighter.'

'So I recall. Your soul burns as bright as any I've seen.' His voice was less harsh now. 'What a waste, hiding behind that silly fence. Join me.' He beckoned, long bony fingers creaking. I was drawn to him, rising from the ground.

'Oi!' Dougie stepped between us, pushing his hands through me. It did the trick. I snapped out of the Lamplighter's spell. Once more, the imprisoned monster hissed.

'Is this how you catch your victims, Lamplighter?' asked Dougie. 'You charm them?'

Neither of us knew a great deal about the Lamplighter's story, only that he supposedly snatched unsuspecting kids from the station back in the day. That was how local legend told it; the truth could be altogether different.

'I make you a promise, boy—'

'*More* promises,' Dougie groaned. He jumped as the flames roared in the Lamplighter's skull, teeth snapping like burned splinters in his jaws.

'So arrogant! I shall enjoy you, when the time comes. For it shall come, I guarantee it, children . . .'

We both shivered, neither of us feeling quite so cocky any more.

'Why have you drawn me from my slumber?'

I looked at Dougie. He looked back. We both shrugged as the Lamplighter watched on expectantly, awaiting our answer.

'We haven't really thought this through, have we?' said Dougie.

'You're the one who rushed down here tonight!'

'OK,' he said, turning back to the apparition. 'What stops you from moving on? Why are you still here, haunting this station?'

'This is my curse.' The Lamplighter sighed, the sharper edges of his dark form softening, the fires in his eyes dying slowly to embers. 'My sins come with a cost. I remain here for eternity.'

'Eternity?' I gasped and pointed at Dougie. 'Does that mean I'll be cursed to follow him around until he's an old man who can't even wipe his bum?'

'Each spirit has its own purpose, its own curse. Mine is to hunt in the dark. I may leave when another takes my place.'

'Another takes your place?' I stifled a grim chuckle. 'I should imagine passing on the stovepipe and staff's a hard sell for anyone.'

'As I said, child,' whispered the Lamplighter. 'An eternity.'

He began to disintegrate before our eyes, his body losing its integrity as curls of dark smoke broke away from his torso. The eyes were pin-pricks now as he dissipated, wisps of black mist carried away on the wind.

'I'll be seeing you, children, soon enough . . .'

Then he was gone, the platform lamps blinking out with his passing. Dougie and I remained where we were, each chilled to the bone.

'I shouldn't need to say this,' said Dougie, 'but we should both agree now. We're *never* coming back to this station. Right?'

Some questions didn't need answering.

ELEVEN

Memories and Masquerades

'This is it,' I said, staring down the overgrown garden path. It was good to be investigating in daylight, the Lamplighter encounter firmly behind us. The sun blazed overhead, the summer heatwave unrelenting, the bungalow's lawn scorched dry. Brambles buttressed up against the brickwork, one enormous rhododendron bush threatening to break down the front door.

'It doesn't look good,' said Dougie. 'It's verging on derelict. Are you sure she still lives here?'

I nodded. 'Last known address according to the census records Andy dug up. After you, pal. Work your charms!'

'I'm a bit self-conscious, turning up alone like this. Should've brought a girl along.'

'You could've always asked Lucy,' I said. 'I don't know why

you continue keeping my existence from her. There was a time when you told her you were being haunted by me, remember?'

'I did, but I think she's pushed it from her mind, dismissed it as a moment of madness.'

'Madness?'

'She probably thought I'd gone off the rails for a while, went a bit ga-ga.'

'Aye. Losing a loved one can do funny things to you.'

'Loved one?' said Dougie, rolling his eyes as he walked down the garden path. 'Self-praise is no recommendation.'

Dougie rapped on the door with his knuckles and waited. There were voices within, footsteps approaching before the door swung open inwards. A squat middle-aged lady stood before us, wearing a navy-blue nurse's uniform. Her grey hair was scraped back from her forehead, her face fixed in a suspicious frown. She looked Dougie up and down. 'Can I help you?'

We'd been expecting to see a frail Mrs Hershey, not a heavy-set district nurse. Dougie's cheeks flushed with colour as he failed to answer.

'You're Ruby's grandson,' I said hastily. 'Scratch that – *great*-grandson!'

'I've come to see Great-Grandma Ruby,' Dougie blurted out, before smiling awkwardly.

'Crikey!' said the nurse with surprise. 'You'd better come in then, hadn't you? This'll make your gran's day, bless her.' She stood aside, allowing Dougie to squeeze past, and called through toward the back of the house. 'Ruby, love. It's your great-grandson here to see you. I'm just getting my gear from the car.'

Then the nurse was off, stomping up the garden path as Dougie crept through the bungalow. He tugged at his T-shirt collar.

'God, I thought it was hot out there, it's stifling in here.'

'Old folk. They'd wear woolly jumpers at the gates of hell.'

Ruby was sat in an armchair in the back room beside a pair of patio doors that overlooked her back garden. Wild though the front garden was, the rear was another world. A carefully tended lawn was bordered by flowers and shrubs of every colour. A wrought-iron bird table stood on the paved area closest to the doors, seed balls and feeders hanging from its edges and eaves. Tits, yellowhammers and a solitary robin jockeyed for position, filling their happy beaks with whatever they could snaffle.

Ruby Hershey turned to face Dougie, her expression a mixture of curiosity and confusion. 'I may be old, but I think I'd recognise my own great-grandchildren. Who are you?'

She was ancient-looking, shrivelled and shrunken within her chair. She wore a tartan blanket over her lap that went all the way down to her slippers, even though it was a glorious summer's day. Her eyes twinkled, belying her years, hinting at mischief and merriment. I imagined her as a young lady, and how hard the Major must have fallen for her.

'I think you'd best tell her, mate,' I said, 'before the nurse returns.'

And so, Dougie did. He wasted little time, all too aware that the medical worker could be back at any moment, screwing up our plans. The story was hokum. He said he was investigating the air base for a school history project over the holidays, her name having popped up in his research. He wanted to record her recollections about the base and the Americans who had lived there. She seemed to buy it. Certain details were spared, such as the fact he knew the Major, who'd been a ghost for seventy years.

Dougie held a dictaphone out before Mrs Hershey, catching every word she imparted. She spoke of the fleets of bombers that soared over the town, the jeeps and trucks that thundered along the cobbled streets. She sighed as she recounted the dance halls where the Yanks courted the local girls. She giggled as she recalled the thrill of nylon stockings, lipstick and chocolate bars, gifted to them by smitten servicemen. She smiled as she was transported back to happier times. We could hear the district nurse in the kitchen, singing to herself, keeping busy.

'And you fell for one of the Americans yourself?' asked Dougie.

'Oh, I did,' she said sweetly, holding her bony hands to her bosom. 'I did indeed.'

Dougie glanced my way hopefully as he continued. 'I saw that you married one, Mrs Hershey.'

Her smile slipped, the look of love shifting to sadness. 'Josh was a good man. Too good for me.'

'Too good? Why would you say that?'

'Because I couldn't give him what he really deserved.'

'You were married, weren't you?'

She stifled a tear, her smile slack as she looked across the room. We followed her gaze to a faded photo above the fireplace. I stepped over to better see it; the American and his bride a vision in sepia, stood in front of the very recognisable St Mary's church.

'We were husband and wife for fifty-two years. Can you believe that?'

'Why you would say Mr Hershey was too good for you?' repeated Dougie, where he knelt beside her chair.

'He deserved better,' said Ruby with a peg-toothed smile. 'I gave him fifty-two years as his faithful wife. I gave him two children. They gave us grandchildren and more. And they're all gone now, too. My son lives in Australia, while my daughter moved to London thirty years ago. And Josh is gone, God bless him. Gone, but not forgotten. He was a good man. But I could never truly give him my love.'

'Why's that?' asked Dougie, though we knew the answer.

'My heart belonged to another,' Ruby whispered.

'So,' said Dougie, inching inexorably toward the tricky subject, 'what happened? The one you loved – why didn't you marry him?'

'The base took a lucky hit, or an unlucky one as the case might be,' she said bitterly. 'A Luftwaffe bomber on its way home from a blitz over Liverpool. They reckoned it was ditching its payload, dropping whatever it hadn't unloaded over us. A dozen died in all. One chap held on until they got him to the hospital ...'

'That's how he died,' I whispered. To see this woman sat before us, clearly still hurting after all these apparently *loveless* years was heartbreaking. 'We should go,' I said, and Dougie nodded in agreement.

'Mrs Hershey,' my friend said. 'Thank you for letting me speak with you today, I really do appreciate it. Would you mind awfully if I returned? There's a few things I'd like to investigate further. Your story's fascinating.'

The nurse stepped through the door into the back room, as Dougie deftly hid the dictaphone back in his pocket.

'Aw,' she said. 'What a lovely surprise, such a smashing kid coming round to see you, eh? You've got a cracking great-grandchild there! You should be very proud.'

'I am,' said Ruby, untucking a handkerchief from her cardigan sleeve and drying her eyes. 'I'm very lucky.'

'Sorry if I upset you,' said Dougie.

'Don't mind me, lovely,' sniffed Ruby. 'These are happy tears. You've made an old lady very happy today. It's nice to reminisce. Nobody asks to hear these stories any more. I don't get many visitors, as you might imagine.'

Dougie rose and said his goodbyes, keeping the charade going with the district nurse until we were out of the bungalow and earshot. Each of us was numb. We walked along the road in silence for a while, lost in our own thoughts. I finally broke the deadlock.

'What do we do? Do we tell the Major that she's loved him all this time?'

'I honestly can't say. It seems that's what we're supposed to do. But how can telling a friend something so cruel be the right thing?'

I couldn't answer his question. Who could? The sun was shining high overhead, the summer sky blue and unspoiled, but dark clouds gathered in our minds.

TWELVE

Pride and Joy

It's fair to say that Dougie and I had been on an emotional rollercoaster of late. Our friendship had experienced its ups and downs, falling apart in the face of accusation and anger. Slowly it was recovering, our trust gradually returning as we faced adversity side by side. Other friendships would have fallen to the wayside, but not Dougie and I. That said, I still wasn't going to hang around in the bathroom while he showered. We were friends, but there were limits.

I waited on the landing as Dougie disappeared into the shower, cleaning himself up after a hot, humid and slightly harrowing day. The encounter with Ruby Hershey had left us both emotionally bruised. We hadn't expected the old lady's words to be quite so touching, her tale of lost love so tragic. It had only served to remind Dougie of how important Lucy was to him. He'd called her, telling her not to make plans for the evening. And so we found ourselves at Casa Hancock, my friend preparing for a hastily arranged date as I killed time at the top of the stairs.

I heard Dougie's dad downstairs, re-entering the kitchen from the garage, the creaking door revealing his location. I drifted downstairs, still in easy reach of my friend but free to wander the house. The bottles clinked against one another as Mr Hancock heeled the garage door closed. More clinking as he fumbled with the key, locking the garage behind him. I watched as he pocketed the key into his crumpled corduroy pants before shuffling back into the lounge. Just how much stinking booze did he keep in there? I phased through the locked garage door to find out.

An Aladdin's cave of junk materialised as I stepped through the barrier. A sliver of light marked the main garage door, the sun's setting rays cutting through the dusty atmosphere like a laser beam. Shelves crowded the walls, overloaded with all manner of paraphernalia. Half-used tins of paint were piled atop one another, jam-jars full of washers and boxes of broken timber loaded up around them. An old bed frame stood on its end along one wall, dust sheets trailing from it like hanging moss. A collection of mops, brushes, garden forks and spades made for an unusual sculpture to the side of the door, threatening to topple over with the slightest jostle. Mr Hancock's old

Bentley took up the lion's share of the garage, his pride and joy at rest in its lair.

'And there's the poison.'

The crates were stacked, bottles of ale that would keep Mr Hancock in a half-cut state for the foreseeable future. He had no intention to quit the demon; its claws were in deep. Was Dougie aware of how much booze there was down there? Grocery deliveries came in the daytime, when Dougie was at school, and the garage was the sole domain of Mr Hancock. He guarded that key like it was the One Ring, never letting it out of his sight. Such was his shame for the arsenal of alcohol he kept in the garage.

It was so sad to see how far Mr Hancock had fallen. When I was little, he'd often looked after me, arranging play dates for Dougie and me while my folks were at work. He was like an uncle, entertaining us for hours on end during those holidays. That was the luxury of being self-employed, only driving when he had to, when clients demanded it. The Bentley always featured in those childhood memories, Dougie and I sat in the back as we travelled in style to the coast or through the Peaks and Dales, windows down. It was such a shame that it now sat in this darkened tomb, gathering dust.

I passed through the Bentley from its rear – metal, wood and upholstery providing no obstacle – before settling into the driver's seat. I was instantly transported back to those road trips. Dougie had lost his mother when he was little, Mr Hancock acting as Dad *and* Mum to his son, providing everything a growing boy needed. Two boys were stashed in the back and the picnic basket would drive up front beside Mr Hancock. *Queen's Greatest Hits* would invariably be playing on the old cassette machine, Freddie and the gang accompanying us on each adventure. We knew those old songs off by heart, father, son and friend singing in not-terribly-perfect harmony as we toured the north together.

I let my hand roll over the steering wheel, imagining its feel, fingertips lingering over the old stereo. A crack in the windscreen rode up the driver's side from the dashboard, no doubt reparable. The walnut dash was coated with grime, long forgotten and ignored. What a waste. This vehicle was a collector's piece. With a bit of TLC the Bentley could be returned to its former glory. What better project to bring father and son together again? In that moment I set my mind to the task. I'd have words with Dougie, sow the seed that this was something they could enjoy. How could Mr Hancock resist? The old car would be the perfect catalyst for good. As the Bentley was brought back to life, so too would Mr Hancock return to his splendour. I could see it now. I clapped my hands like a giddy schoolgirl fixing friends up on a date. I'd be their fairy godmother!

I made a mental note of what needed doing. I was out of the door and inspecting the exterior bodywork, carrying out a ghostly MOT. It was mostly cosmetic, spit and polish needed here and there. Beneath the dust, the car was in as fine a shape as ever. I lingered at the boot, blanching as I recalled the time Dougie had accidentally locked himself in there. We were nine years old and playing hide and seek, my friend ducking into the Bentley in search of the perfect hiding place. It had been an hour until I found him, and I'd been unable to spring the lock. Mr Hancock had been furious to discover his son trapped. That taught us two things that day. Firstly, never climb inside anything mechanical when playing hide and seek. Ever. Secondly, leave Mr Hancock's car alone. Always. Since then, the garage had been strictly off limits to Dougie.

I drifted around the car, almost completing my circuit. I wondered if Dougie was out of the shower yet, how he would take to my suggestion of them working on the Bentley together. I was back around the passenger's side now, approaching the front wing. Perhaps we could take it for a spin again, hit the road once more. The car hadn't left the garage in months. Thinking about it for a moment, I couldn't recall an occasion I'd seen it in daylight since I'd been a ghost. Not since I'd become a ghost.

It hit me all at once, creeping up from nowhere, taking me

by surprise. The crack in the windscreen was the first clue, but blissfully, perhaps willingly, ignored. My spirits had been soaring seconds ago, but now a sickness washed over me in a tidal wave. As I looked down at the passenger's wing of the Bentley, the world tilted. My vision was screwed, everything fractured, as if viewed through a kaleidoscope. I tried to blink the confusion away, regain my balance, but it was hopeless. I stared at the car in horror.

The Bentley's bodywork was in fine shape, no doubt, all except that wing and the very front of the car. There was the crack in the glass, a jagged lightning bolt that tore through the windscreen. A great dint had battered the bonnet out of shape, the sheet metal staved in. The panel around the wheel arch was bent and buckled, paint scuffed and peeling. I fell to my knees, shuddering, refusing to make sense of the damning evidence before my eyes. If I could've vomited, I would have. If I wasn't dead, I could've died all over again.

Flakes of electric blue were caught within the Bentley's black paint, shining like sparks in the darkness. The electric blue of my mountain bike; unmissable, unmistakable. I tried to scramble away, but I was drawn to the car like a ghoul to a crash. I had no heart, no blood, no veins or arteries, yet my head thundered, great booms shaking my soul to its core. Beyond that storm, the *Coronation Street* theme tune played, distant, drab and discordant. He was in there watching his television, drinking his booze, drowning his sorrows. He was in there.

My friend's father.

My killer.

THIRTEEN

Cornettos and Conundrums

I said nothing to Dougie. I mean, really; what *could* I possibly say?

He met up with Lucy that night and, as ever, I drifted along in silence behind them. They went to the usual haunts, if you'll pardon the pun – the playground, the canal, the old school field – and I kept my distance, lost in my dark thoughts. I bore them no ill will but although I'd promised him I'd be cheery and positive henceforth, here was my first chance to come good on that vow, and I was apparently in a mood again. I was numb, with nowhere to turn.

Dougie turned in that night unsure of what was wrong with me. Little was said. We'd been through so much lately that he hadn't bothered pressing me on it, but I could tell he was disappointed. He probably thought I was jealous.

Nothing was further from the truth. The sad fact was, I couldn't look at him without wanting to tell him what I knew. How could I break something like that to him? I knew his father's secret and I couldn't share it. Could I? It would break him.

While Dougie slept, I prowled. I returned to the garage on countless occasions, wanting it to have all been some hideous nightmare. The flecks of blue paint awaited me on each occasion, reminding me it was all too terribly real. And Mr Hancock? He finally sloped off to bed in the early hours, falling into a fitful sleep. It was Dougie I usually kept watch over with only the stars for company. Not this night. I watched over Mr Hancock, monitored the rise and fall of his chest. I saw him toss and turn. I hoped his nightmares were vivid.

The next day we headed to the hospital. We had an appointment with the Major, set upon telling him Ruby's whereabouts. That information was the last thing on my mind that morning, as Dougie recounted what we'd discovered. We were back in the rose garden, surrounded by dressing-gowned patients and bouquet-bearing loved ones. The Major listened on in silence as Dougie told him what he knew. Occasionally he looked my way, clearly aware of my funk and no doubt wondering what had transpired.

'She never got over you,' said Dougie. 'All those years,

married to your mate, Josh, and it was you she still loved. Sorry, pal.'

'But she had kids, right? And grandkids and so forth? She found happiness, surely?'

'She was happy, and no doubt loved her family, but not in the way in which she loved you. I guess loving someone and being "in love" are different things.'

'Steady, Sparky, you almost sounded profound there for a moment. Had me worried.' Dougie smiled, but none of us felt like laughing.

'What will you do?' asked my mate.

The Major shrugged. 'There's not much I can do. This is where I belong. The hospital's my home, kid.'

'Is there nothing we can do for you? You never got the chance to say goodbye. Perhaps that's what's kept you here, those unspoken words, those unshared feelings. We know about the bomb that hit the base. The one that got you. Let us help you guys. I don't mind passing a message on to her, Chip.'

'You called me by my proper name, Sparky!'

'Don't get used to it,' Dougie replied. 'Tell us. How can we help?'

The American thought for a moment, that rare, serious look returning. 'That newspaper article said they're demolishing the base. Perhaps—'

'Hold that thought,' said Dougie, cutting the Major's speech short as an unusual van pulled up outside the A&E. 'I'm off for a Cornetto.'

'That's an ambulance, Sparky!'

'Funny guy,' Dougie called back as he scampered off after the ice-cream van.

'Go on then,' said the Major to me. 'Out with it. What's got you down in the dumps, kid? You gotta face like a bulldog licking whizz off a nettle.'

Where to begin? I wondered. I watched as Dougie arrived beside the ice-cream van and took his place, queuing in the sunshine.

'It was his dad.'

'Come again? Whose dad did what?'

'The car that hit me. Dougie's father was driving it. Mr Hancock killed me.'

The Major exhaled, long and slow. He scratched his head, messing up that majestic, jet-black quiff.

'You're sure of this?'

'Deadly sure,' I replied. The words caught in my throat. I felt dizzy, lightheaded, my gaze never leaving Dougie as he waved at us. I raised a trembling hand in acknowledgement. Opening up to the Major felt cathartic, like I'd let the genie out of the bottle, but there was no coaxing it back in now.

'I found his car in the garage. The damage all tied in to the night of the accident. He hasn't driven it and he's been drinking himself into an early grave in the meantime. I even found the paint from my bicycle grazed into the bodywork. It was Mr Hancock alright. I knew he was keeping a secret – he'd mentioned as much in a phone call I overhead – but I would never have imagined it was this. He *killed me,* for goodness' sake! What do I do, Chip? What do I do?'

'Steady, kid,' he said, patting my knee. 'Just relax. If what you say is true—'

'It is!'

'OK, so it's true, but you need to keep your emotions in check. Sparky over there'll be picking up your bad juju. You're giving off a mortifying vibe at the minute – hell, even I can feel it – and if you don't want your buddy cottoning on, you need to get a grip, pronto!'

I tried to compose myself, but it was just so damned hard. After suspecting I'd never discover the identity of my killer, all of a sudden *there he was,* and he'd been under my nose the whole time!

'I'm sorry,' I whispered, refocusing my energies. 'Can you help me?'

'Will, you need to ask yourself: what it is you *want* to do?'

I considered it for a moment. 'I want justice, I think.'

'Justice? We talking eye for an eye? You want him dead?'

The thought hadn't even occurred to me, and there it was,

out in the open. How would I do it? Would I use the push, give him a shove from the top of the stairs? I shivered, trying to imagine being responsible for the taking of another's life. I'd played my part in the demise of the old headmaster, Mr Goodman, which ultimately led to him falling to his death in Red Brook House. But that wicked old sod had brought about his own end. Right at the last I'd even tried to save him, but to no avail. What the Major now suggested was a world away from the events of that sorry night.

'No,' I said. 'That's not me, and never will be. Regardless of what he did, I couldn't dish out the same. But he needs to answer for his crime.'

'Tell your pal, then.'

I shook my head. 'I couldn't possibly.'

'I thought we said you needed to be straight with your mates from now on? You said you would be, remember?'

'But that? *"Hey, guess what, mate; your old man's the murdering swine who killed me."*'

'I'm not sure what options you're left with, kid,' said the Major sadly.

I clenched my fists, thinking of what I might do if I were angry enough. I kept returning to the push, and what other tricks I might utilise. Perhaps I *could* haunt Mr Hancock? I'd read about poltergeists, had a pretty good handle on how they worked. I could let rip in the living room, knock the place to hell, break everything that's breakable including his cursed beer bottles. Maybe I could bang the car in the garage, pummel it with my fists until he *had* to come through and face his crime, *had* to witness my anger, *had* to act upon his guilty conscience.

'I've got it,' I said, my voice assured now. 'I'm going to give him the fright of his life. If that doesn't persuade him to confess, nothing will.'

'Attaboy, kid,' said the American, patting my back. 'See, you're even thinking like a ghost now. I'm proud of ya!'

I watched Dougie unpeeling the wrapper from his Cornetto. He took a great lick.

'This is going to break his heart,' I said.

'The truth must come out, Will. People should answer for their crimes.'

'You know what this means?' I said quietly as my friend began to walk back to us. 'I got it all so wrong. I thought I was here because of Dougie. All this time, I imagined it was our friendship that had stopped me moving on. I thought it was the love of two best mates that kept me by his side. It wasn't at all, though. The night of my funeral when I turned up at Dougie's house, I misread why I'd been drawn there. I got the wrong end of the stick, mistakenly latching on to my friend, but it wasn't him I was supposed to be haunting. It was his father.'

Dougie smiled as he drew nearer, his chin dripping with ice cream and raspberry ripple sauce. My voice was a whisper in the Major's ear, my words heavy with horrible realisation.

'It's Mr Hancock I've been haunting all along.'

FOURTEEN

Victims and Vengeance

I sat in the shadows, watching Dougie sleep. His breathing had levelled out just before midnight. The witching hour. How appropriate. We joked about my loitering around his room through the night, staring at him as he slept, with nothing better to do. There were no giggles to be had this evening, though. Finally content that he'd hit a deep sleep, I rose from the foot of his bed.

'Sorry about this, mate,' I whispered, moving on and through the bedroom door.

I flitted across the landing to Mr Hancock's bedroom. I let my anger grow, casting my mind back to the night of my death, my emotions building toward a crescendo. That strange, ghostly power pulsing through me, ready to be channelled into a show of frightening revenge. I stepped through the door.

It was the master bedroom, spacious because of the house having been built before the war. Upon inspection, it appeared to be still stuck in that era. The room looked like a bomb had hit it, cupboard doors open, drawers spewing clothes on to the carpet. Garments littered the floor and bed, clean and soiled alike, but there was no sign of Dougie's dad.

I drifted downstairs, heading toward the lounge. The television sent lights dancing and flickering across the dappled glass panel in the door. I could hear the steady *rat-tat-tat-tat* of machine gunfire, as whatever war film Mr Hancock was watching broke the silence of the night. I paused at the door, refocusing my emotions once again. The man who killed me was in that room, waiting for me, oblivious to the forthcoming scare. It was long overdue. I glanced at my hands, each curled into a fist and radiating a strange blue light. Despite my anger, I felt a calm settle over me. What I was about to do was wholly righteous. This was the *only* thing to do. I phased through the glass panel and into the lounge.

It wasn't a war film on the telly. Instead, I was greeted by Jimmy Cagney, his tommy-gun spitting lead into a mob of gangsters. The Major would've approved. The stack of bottles had grown some since earlier that evening, but again, there was no sign of my killer. He'd spent the last six months closeted away inside this house, in this very room, in *that stinking chair,* and now he was gone? Surely he couldn't have picked tonight to finally haul himself out of the front door and into the fresh air? Whatever sympathy I'd had for Mr Hancock had vanished the moment I realised his crime. The man who had looked after me as a nipper was dead to me. It was only Dougie I cared about now.

'Where are you?' I muttered, stepping up to the living-room window and sticking my head through the curtains and glass.

There was nobody in the street. The lights in the neighbours' houses were off for the night. A solitary street lamp stood at the top of Dougie's little close where it met the main road, but the bottom of the cul-de-sac remained in darkness. That is, except for the thin beam of illumination that leaked out from around the Hancock's garage door. I drew my head back into the lounge.

Out of habit, I took the winding route through the house to get to the door into the garage. I could've just headed straight there, but it gave me more time to think, to consider what I was going to do. If anything, having him trapped in the garage like a rat in a barrel was even better. There was all manner of hard and heavy objects I could topple over in there. Tins of paint, glass jars, bottles, brooms and bedheads; he'd think the ceiling was coming down by the time I was finished. And there, right before his murderous miserable face, would be the car. The car that killed me. This would break him. He would *have* to go to the police. I took a deep breath in the kitchen, wavering before the garage door. This was going to work. I stepped through.

He was sat on an upturned crate, a bottle in hand (of course), his back turned to the door. His free hand clutched the thinning hair on top of his head, the elbow digging into his knee, his body a slumped bag of bones. A bare bulb lit the garage, hanging from the rafters above the Bentley.

I'd no idea how long he'd been in here; Dougie had turned in early, ten-thirty, catching Lucy on Skype before hitting the pillow. Mr Hancock had still been in the lounge. He'd clearly waited for his son to disappear before shuffling into the garage.

I stared at his back, his crumpled clothes hanging off him. I'd no sense of smell, but I didn't need one. I imagined he reeked of body odour and booze, his world a miserable, lonely one. He cut a desperately pathetic figure. I looked around the garage, spying the ephemera and clutter that I could use upon him. I was spoiled for choice; where to begin? Hit the paint shelves? Push over the toolbox? Knock the man over where he sat? Or maybe cut straight to the chase and strike the battered bonnet of his beloved Bentley?

Those fists were shaking now, my chest constricting as my rage boiled up. I was here to scare him, to shake him up, to shame him into doing the right thing, but at that moment all

I saw was revenge. I'd convinced myself that wasn't me, that I could never hurt a living soul. Only I wasn't a living soul any more, was I? He'd put paid to that. He'd cut my life short before it had really begun. Before I knew it, both of my fists had risen into the air, high above Mr Hancock where he slumped on his crate, head in hand. They were bright white now, twin beacons of just fury about to descend. And then he spoke.

'I know you're there, Will.'

I faltered, my focus thrown. Did he *really* just say that? I stepped back unsteadily, fists unclenching, the bright light fading in my palms. How could he see me? Scratch that; how *long* had he been able to see me for? All this time? Since I died? The tables had turned suddenly, the element of surprise gone, and I had no idea how to react. My confidence leaked away, as swiftly as blood from a knife wound.

'You can *see* me?' I hissed.

'I just hope you're listening, lad,' said Mr Hancock, lifting his bottle in the direction of the Bentley and sloshing its contents about. 'You know, it's been a while since we last chatted.'

'A while? Try autumn. Around the time you killed me.'

He didn't respond to my barbed comment, rambling along his own train of thought. 'Dougie copes, but it must be difficult. I guess that girl Lizzie helps.'

'Lucy,' I corrected him.

'Lucy,' he clicked his fingers. 'She must take his mind off you not being there. Not met her yet myself.'

'She's lovely,' I whispered. The anger simmered, but my scheme had stuttered to a halt. The last thing I'd envisaged was being drawn into a conversation.

'I don't suppose he's in a hurry to introduce her to me. I mean, look at me. I'm a bloody shambles. I've let him down. He'd be better off without me.'

'Do the right thing, Mr Hancock,' I said. The words caught in my throat as I found myself trying to reason with him. 'Turn yourself in. Confess to what you did. That's the only way you'll regain your son's trust.'

Dougie's dad reached forward and ran his fingertips along the buckled metal wing of the Bentley. He flinched as he touched it, before flattening his palm against the busted bodywork. 'I haven't driven this car since it happened. I couldn't even bring myself to take it to the garage, get it fixed. I'm afraid they'll ask me what happened, and I know I won't be able to lie.'

'Then don't lie. Tell the truth!'

'I'll start blabbing, and blubbing, and I won't be able to stop.' He was sobbing now. He took a swig from the bottle and shook his head. 'I'm so sorry, Will. So very sorry. I think I've cried out all my tears, but there's always more.'

'Call the police, Mr Hancock. Explain what happened.'

His laughter was sudden and harsh. 'You know what, Will? You know what I'd give anything for? A moment. Just one moment where I got to say sorry to you for what happened that night, for the part I played in it.' The bottle tumbled out of his hand and skittered across the floor. It rolled to a halt beneath the Bentley. 'Only I'll never get that chance.'

I was confused. I manoeuvred around him to look at his face. He was staring at the twisted wheel arch, his eyes not even registering as I loomed into view. Wait, he *couldn't* see me? I waved my hand in front of his face. Still nothing. 'Mr Hancock?' No reaction. I'm not being funny, but that would've been a poop-hot trick to ignore a glowing blue teenage boy doing jazz hands in your face.

I stood up, suddenly realising that I hadn't been taking part in a conversation at all. I'd just witnessed a monologue, a rambling confession from a drunken man to a battered old car. He was bumping his gums now, muttering about how sorry he was, the words growing more incoherent.

I backed up, drifting to the kitchen door, unable to look at Mr Hancock any more. I phased through the wood, out of the grim light of the garage and into the cold gloom of the kitchen. It changed nothing. He still needed to confess. But the hate I felt for him was gone now, replaced by pity. I saw him for what he was, a foolish, weak man incapable of doing the right thing. He'd need convincing, still, but a heart-attack-inducing fright wasn't the answer any more. I needed help.

I needed Dougie.

FIFTEEN

Out and Open

'Just open the door.'

Dougie shook his head as the milk cascaded over his cornflakes. 'There's a reason it's off limits, Will. I won't disobey him.'

'And what reason could that possibly be? A giant mousetrap? An angry hippo? Ravenous flying monkeys? Why on earth are you banned from your own garage? Ask yourself.'

I was angry. I'd spent half an hour trying to persuade him that there was something really important in there that he *had* to see with his own eyes. But he was having none of it, sticking his head in the sand and hoping I'd stop pestering him. That wasn't happening any time soon.

'Things are shaky enough between me and him at the moment,' said Dougie, returning the milk to the fridge. 'I don't want to rock the boat any further.'

Rock the boat? If he thought things were rough now he didn't know the half of it. My anger was building, threatening to explode. He must have suspected this was bigger than anything we'd previously discussed. He must have *felt* my anxiety.

'The door, Dougie.' I struggled to keep my irritation in check.

'I don't even have the key,' he said, taking the first mouthful of cereal from his bowl.

'Then go get it. He's asleep in his armchair. He never made it to bed last night. It's in his pocket.'

'What? I'm just a common thief now who steals things from my drunken old man?'

'Please,' I said, my head splitting, vision blurring. 'Open the garage door. There's something *really* important you need to see.'

'I know he keeps his drink in there, Will. I don't need to see that bottle tower.'

'Just open it!' I shouted, slamming my fist against the lock with all my might. The handle juddered, the wood splintered and the door swung open. Dougie and I stared at the broken lock in shock.

'Oh, you've done it now,' said Dougie, cornflakes tumbling from his mouth on to the breakfast counter. 'He's going to *kill* me!'

Blue light pulsed through the flesh of my hand. 'Umm . . .

That'll probably come out of your allowance. But, on the bright side, we no longer need the key.' I stood to one side (quite unnecessarily) and gestured through the open door toward the garage. 'Trust me, Dougie. You need to see this.'

'Dad. Wake up.'

Mr Hancock stirred in his armchair, a dishevelled, unshaven mess. He sat forward, crumpled clothes clinging to his creaking bones. He rubbed his eyes with the ball of his fists, squinting as he checked the carriage clock on the mantelpiece.

'What time is it?'

'Morning, Dad. You need to wake up. Now. We have to talk.'

Dougie stood over his father, his face hard, jaw clenched. He looked down his nose at him, unblinking. There was revulsion in his gaze; disgust and disappointment all rolled into one. I could tell by his voice he was just about keeping it together. It was taking every ounce of his willpower not to reach forward and throttle the man. If my aura was ghostly blue, then Dougie's was furious red, a fire about to be unleashed.

'I have to sleep, son,' said Mr Hancock, collapsing back into his chair.

'You're done sleeping. You need to talk.'

His father forced his blood-red eyes wide, straining with the effort. His gaze drifted to Dougie's hand, specifically the object he held.

'What have you got there?'

Dougie threw the telephone handset on to the sofa.

'I've just called the police. They'll be here soon enough. You need to start talking. Now.'

Mr Hancock spluttered, his mask of confusion twisting awkwardly into one of amusement. He stifled a weird laugh. 'What are you talking about, son?'

'You need to talk to me before the police get here. Come clean now, Dad. Quit lying.'

Wow. I hadn't been expecting Dougie to come out all guns blazing. When he saw the damaged car and the unmistakable, irrefutable evidence, he'd become a statue for ten minutes. I'd been unable to get through to him, my words falling on deaf ears as he stared at the beaten-up Bentley. I'd half-feared he was going to lose it, fly into a wild temper that brought the whole garage down around him. But he simply hit the pause button, freeze-framed in horror.

'I don't know what you mean about lies, Douglas, but you—'

'The car, Dad. Tell me about the car.'

Mr Hancock fell silent. His face was always pale, but at that moment he looked like a ghost. The irony wasn't lost on me.

'You've been in the garage?' His voice was barely audible.

'You sound *surprised,* Dad.'

Dougie's lips curled. I placed my hand on his shoulder, trying to keep him calm, pushing ever so slightly to remind him I was by his side.

'Go easy, pal,' I said. 'Give him a chance to answer. Hear what he has to say.'

Dougie took a breath. 'The car, Dad. The truth. The night of Will's death. Tell me.'

Mr Hancock reached a trembling hand toward the bottles beside his chair.

'You have *got* to be kidding?' said Dougie, taking a step forward. At that moment I was convinced that, should his father pick up a beer, my friend would have kicked it clean from his hand. Thankfully Mr Hancock thought better of it.

'You called the police?' His voice trembled, fearful.

'God help me, I don't ask for much. I never have. Tell me what happened before they get here.'

A strange thing then happened; Mr Hancock relaxed. Since my death, Dougie's father had gradually transformed from a gentle, kind soul into a wretched, wrinkled mess. Worry lines had etched his face, growing deeper and more furrowed as days turned to weeks then months. The hatch-marks that criss-crossed his brow made him look permanently headache stricken. And now they were gone. At that moment, it was as if the burden had been lifted from his shoulders. For the first time in forever he was himself once more, however fleetingly.

'It's not what you might think, Douglas. Truly, it isn't.'

He closed his eyes, recalling the events of that fateful night. I caught sight of a car drive past the lounge window, down into the bottom of the cul-de-sac where the Hancock house was situated. I peeked my head through the glass and craned my neck to better see; a police car made a three-point turn, pulling up at the head of Dougie's drive. I withdrew into the house.

'It's the cops, Dougie. They're here!'

'Dad, you've a matter of seconds to tell me what went on.' He gestured to the window. 'The police think they're turning up to a domestic. Are they?'

Mr Hancock leaned forward, his voice steady for the first time in months.

'I wasn't driving the Bentley, Douglas.'

'Then how do you explain the damage to the wing? I suppose that was some other blue bicycle it crashed into?'

'No, it was Will Underwood's bicycle.'

I felt sick, hearing him say those words.

'But you deny driving the car?'

'I was a passenger.'

'But it's your car! You're precious about the Bentley. You never let anyone drive it.'

I heard the policeman's footsteps up the gravel drive. Mr Hancock looked suddenly terribly sick.

'I let him.'

'Who?' asked Dougie, but at that moment, I knew.

'Bradbury.'

Dougie swayed unsteadily with the fresh revelation.

'Then why not tell the police that? Why hide the evidence for him?'

'I had no proof to say it was Bradbury. Only my word.'

There was a hammering of a fist at the door; urgent, concerned.

'Your word's not good enough?'

'Not against Bradbury.'

A shout through the letterbox from the policeman, calling for someone to come to the door immediately. Dougie pointed to the hall, his voice a whisper.

'Go and tell them now. Explain what happened.'

Mr Hancock tearfully shook his head.

'If you don't, I will.' Dougie made for the door, but Mr Hancock was out of his chair with a speed that belied his booze-addled state. He caught his son's wrist and yanked him close. He spoke through gritted teeth, his Adam's apple bobbing in his grizzled throat.

'You can't, Douglas. They'll never believe you!'

'I can make them try! We both can.'

Again, a shout from the policeman, now threatening to break down the door. I peered down the hall, the bobby's eyes looking through the brass hatch.

'You don't understand what Bradbury and his friends will do,' said Mr Hancock. 'He's a monster.'

'You're scared of what he'll do to you?'

'No,' Mr Hancock said, tearfully. 'I'm scared of what he'll do to *you*.' He let go of Dougie's wrist as a final warning echoed through the hall, the front door about to feel the full force of an irate policeman's shoulder.

'Do what you must, Douglas,' said his father. 'I'll still love you, regardless.'

Dougie looked from his dad to me. I shrugged, lost for comforting words. What *could* he do? Spill what he knew to the police and face the consequences with Bradbury? That's *if* his father was even telling the truth. And what about me? Where did justice for his murdered friend fit into the equation? No, I had no answers: he was damned either way, whatever he did. I had only the one comment, and it wasn't the most helpful, but it was certainly the most pressing.

'There's somebody at the door.'

SIXTEEN

The Truth and the Terrible

'I really should write this up,' said Sergeant Kramer, flipping his notebook shut and slotting it into his breast pocket.

'I can assure you, Officer,' said Mr Hancock, 'this won't happen again.'

'It had better not. We take hoax calls very seriously down at the station.' He shook his head as he rose from the sofa, Dougie shamefaced on a cushion beside him. 'Wasting police time's a grave offence, lad.'

'I know,' said Mr Hancock, smiling apologetically. 'And I'm sure Douglas understands too, don't you, son?'

Dougie nodded and stared up at the sergeant with admonished, puppy dog eyes. As pitiful looks went, it was a winner.

'Sorry, sir. I don't know what I was thinking.'

'I don't think you were thinking at all.' Suddenly, Sergeant Kramer clicked his fingers. 'You're the kid who survived the attack in the old school house! I knew I recognised the name. That headmaster who went loopy, right?'

Dougie's mask of misery slipped at the mention of Red Brook House. He made headline news that day in autumn, locally and nationally. He'd ridden that tide of celebrity in the following days and weeks, but time had moved on. For many, it was already a dim and distant memory, but it had clearly struck a chord with Sergeant Kramer, who turned to Mr Hancock as he was led into the hall.

'You know, you might want to look into this,' he said, voice low. 'Crazy business what went on at that school house. And to think, the headmaster was behind it? I'm no psychologist but daft calls like what your boy's been up to can be a cry for help. Perhaps there's a shrink he can speak to. Maybe he has issues that have driven him to this, eh?'

'Yes, Sergeant,' said Mr Hancock, opening the front door. 'You may well be on to something there. We'll be sure to arrange for a doctor's appointment at the soonest and talk about that very thing.'

'Just keep an eye on the lad, yeah?' said Kramer. 'You're his dad. If anyone can spot when something's not right, it should be you.'

The door closed and the latch clunked into place. Dougie

and I stood at the window, watching the police car head off. That had taken some explaining, and thankfully Dougie made a good blagger when circumstances demanded. Sergeant Kramer had answered an emergency call, arriving pumped up and braced for violence. When a teenage boy had calmly answered the door, the poor chap had looked rather crestfallen, the energy escaping his tense frame like guff from a whoopee cushion. There had been no domestic, just an apologetic son and an embarrassed father.

'Yeah,' said Dougie, rolling his eyes as his father returned. 'You'll keep watch over me, won't you, Dad?'

'Sorry about that,' said Mr Hancock, standing over his chair and its creased cushions. He scratched his jaw before joining Dougie at the window. He squinted, flinching like a Morlock seeing daylight for the first time. 'Thanks for taking the rap there.'

'It's the only one I will take, Dad. Now might be a good time for you to explain everything that's happened. Remind me why I'm not turning you into the police for the part you played in Will's murder.'

I was taken aback by the choice of words, and so was Dougie's father.

'Hang about, Douglas. Murder's a bit strong!'

'Is it? What happened?'

Mr Hancock turned his back on the bright window. He

dropped his head, chin resting on chest, his haggard face lost in shadow. 'I remember it being deathly cold.'

I shivered, the irony of the phrase not lost on me, as Dougie's dad continued.

'I hadn't been expecting a call from him. I'd been playing dominoes with the lads at the social club. When the phone rang there was no avoiding him; you don't dodge Bradbury. It's just not done. So I took the call and did I as I was told. He needed picking up from a business appointment at the snooker hall.'

'Which one?' asked Dougie.

'Behind the rugby club.'

I knew the place well, and so did Dougie, the two of us sharing a look. We knew *not* to go there. It was in a rough part of town, a well known hangout for bad lads. Most of the pubs and nightclubs in town hired their bouncers from that snooker hall, a breeding ground for knuckle-dragging Neanderthals.

'That place is always in the news,' said Dougie. 'Somebody's always getting beaten up there.'

'That night was no different,' said Mr Hancock. 'Turns out the business Bradbury had there was a spot of retribution.'

'Retribution?'

'Aye. Some deal he had turned sour. I found him skulking in the shadows outside, sporting that spivvy black suit, canvas bag slung across his shoulder, nursing bloody knuckles.'

‘He beat somebody up?’

‘Oh yes. He was forever doing that.’

‘I thought he was the Big I Am? Doesn’t he have friends to do that stuff for him?’

‘He has hired thugs for sure, but you’re missing something important here, son; Bradbury *likes* that side of his job. He *enjoys* getting his fists dirty.’

‘So he beat some guy up that night?’

‘A couple of guys actually. Unpaid debts apparently. That’s what was in the holdall, a heap of cash. He wanted me to take him to his lock-up, then home. I should’ve taken him straight home, right there and then. I could sense his blood was up and he reeked of booze. Last thing I wanted to do was tick him off, so I drove him to his lock-up.’

I tried to imagine Mr Hancock’s anxiety in Bradbury’s presence. Dougie and I had met the man, of course, the day we were chased through town by Vinnie Savage. Sunshine has a way of softening those harsh and horrid edges in life, dialling down the potential terror of a situation. But Bradbury had scared us both. He had an assured, confident menace.

‘I must have waited for fifteen minutes outside the lock-up for him to come back out. I was having a leak in the bushes when he finally reappeared and by the time I got back to the Bentley he was sitting in it. In the driver’s seat.’

Mr Hancock shivered in spite of the sunlight upon his

back. Dougie's face glistened, his brow slick with sweat as he followed his father's confession. His nerve impressed me. Had the roles been reversed, I doubted I could've stood there as my old man spilled his guts. I'd have left the room, unable to look at him, let alone listen. But my mate stayed put, feet fixed to the carpet as if nailed there. Mr Hancock caught his breath, composing himself.

'I should've said something; insisted he move across, allow me to drive. But who am I kidding? Nobody speaks to Bradbury that way. I took the passenger seat he'd vacated and he pulled the Bentley away from the lock-up.'

Again, Mr Hancock paused. 'That ride . . . if I close my eyes, I can see it, now. Bradbury cursing his enemies, barking out obscenities, swerving across the road. He was all over the shop. I tried reaching, to straighten the steering wheel, keep him from driving into oncoming traffic.'

He stopped to clear his throat. 'The bicycle . . . I saw its lights, I shouted at Bradbury, tried to warn him. All he heard was my yelling as I hit his hands away, grabbing the wheel. He retaliated, elbowed me in the face, sent me back into my seat. Next moment, we'd hit him.'

'Will, Dad. You hit Will.' Dougie took a protective step closer to me. I swear, if he could've reached out and held my hand, he'd have done so.

'The Bentley's a big car. Powerful. Unforgiving. It took

quite an impact for the bicycle and rider to stave a wing in. The crack on the windscreen where he rode off the bonnet tells its own tale. And you probably couldn't see, but the roof is also dinged where he bounced off it.'

My guts were in knots as he described the events of my death, oblivious to the fact I was stood before him. Perhaps it was the way he reeled off the details in matter-of-fact fashion, like a match report on the evening news. Every impact rushed back, shuddering through my body, causing my very being to hum and vibrate. I could *feel* the accident all over again, my bones breaking, body pulverised. For a moment I thought I might tear apart, right there and then, a smear of ectoplasm my parting shot on the living-room carpet. I swear, if it hadn't been for Dougie's passionate words, I'd have blinked out of existence altogether. Not for the first time, he was my anchor to the world of the living.

'*He*, Dad, you keep saying *he*. It was Will, remember? My best friend!'

Mr Hancock winced, pinching the bridge of his nose. The words found their way out between tear-soaked sobs. 'I relive that journey every bloody night, Douglas. That's my punishment, son. That's my curse.'

'He thinks *he's* cursed,' Dougie whispered under his breath as his father trembled uncontrollably. 'He should try enduring you twenty-four/seven.' It was light-hearted, meant to diffuse the tension I was clearly feeling. My anxiety must have been rolling off me like a tsunami and Dougie took the brunt of every wave. His banter was well meant, but misjudged.

'Let him speak, Dougie.'

We turned back to his wretched dad as he continued. 'He got out of the car at the bottom of the road, left the engine running. Said he'd walk the rest of the way, no longer needed the lift. All I could do was stare back up the street to the top of the rise. I could see the mangled shape on the tarmac, boy and bicycle, buckled wheel still turning and catching the moonlight. I was frozen. Then Bradbury was off, but not before he'd dragged me into the driver's seat and threatened me. It was my car, he said. If *anyone* ever connected him to this night, he'd tell them it was me who was driving. And I'd confess to that very thing if I knew what was good for me. Good for me . . . *and my son.*'

Mr Hancock dropped to his knees, assuming the position of condemned awaiting the executioner's axe. The blood had drained from Dougie's face, leaving him as washed out as a pair of hand-me-down growlers. He searched my face for answers, but what was I to say?

'Dude,' I sighed. 'I think he needs you.'

Dougie tentatively reached a hand forward, palm down, hovering over his father. He seemed unsure of whether to touch him or not, as if he'd catch leprosy with the slightest contact. Finally he patted Mr Hancock's shoulder gingerly, his dad shaking as if electrocuted by his son's compassion.

'Let it out,' said my mate, roles reversed as was so often the case.

His father sobbed, a broken man.

'Just let it out, Dad.'

SEVENTEEN

The Major and the Mission

'Bummer of a deal, Sparky.'

The Major winced, ruffling his immaculate black quiff until it had transformed into a roadkilled crow. Dougie shifted uncomfortably against the wall outside the A&E. If anyone was looking to master the art of standing awkwardly with the weight of the world upon one's shoulders, then my mate had just nailed it.

'Sounds like your old man's been stuck between a rock and a hard place since your best buddy here bought it. Jeez, I wouldn't wish that guilt on my worst enemy.'

'You could wish it on Bradbury,' I said without hesitation. Neither of them disagreed. 'What he's put your dad through, Dougie . . .'

Dougie shook his head. 'He doesn't resemble the man who raised me. He's a mess. And it's all Bradbury's fault.'

'And he isn't finished with him yet,' I added.

'How so?' asked the Major.

'He's lined up Mr Hancock for another job. Apparently this will buy him his freedom from Bradbury.'

'And he can't go to the cops because every bit of evidence points to *him* being behind the wheel. Man, that blows.' The Major sucked his teeth. 'This Bradbury; what kinda guy is he?'

'A very bad one,' I said, doing the villain a great disservice in the description department.

'He's a career criminal,' said Dougie, picking up the story. 'Late thirties and never done an honest day's work in his life, if what Dad says is true.' I thought about my friend's choice of words as he continued; did he doubt Mr Hancock's version of events or was it just a slip of the tongue? 'He was born in Liverpool and moved here as a teenager. Bradbury was a bad lad before he even got here and soon had his own gang running rackets across the borough: robberies, extortion, drugs and loan sharking. Seems there's nowt he won't do to make a few quid.'

'Sounds like a real piece o' work,' said the Major, breathing life into his quiff once more with a few sweeps of his hands.

'He dresses in a snappy black suit, white shirt, black tie. Fashions himself on those old East End gangsters from the Sixties. Or *Reservoir Dogs.* Wears his black hair slicked back.' Dougie turned to the Major. 'Not unlike yours.'

'Back up, Sparky,' said the Major. 'I've been sporting this look since the Forties. Sounds like Bradbury's all about appearances. He's a cheap knock-off, a hokey imitation of a villain.'

'There's nothing fake about him,' I said. 'You can't underestimate him. He's put plenty of people in hospital – you've probably witnessed them rolling through those doors on gurneys – and he's lost no sleep over what happened to me. He's a gangster alright. He's the Real McCoy.'

'I don't know what to say, boys. As you know, when it comes to matters of the heart, I'm your man. If it's lady trouble, look no further. But dealing with killers? I'm striking out. That's what the cops are for, ain't it?'

'Ordinarily, yeah,' agreed Dougie. 'But not when Bradbury's got my old man's knackers in a vice. Dad has no evidence to prove Bradbury was driving that night. Indeed, all *we* have is his word.'

'But that's enough, right?' I asked, wanting to check where my pal stood on his father's innocence.

When Dougie spoke it was with all the integrity his breaking voice could muster. 'I'm in no doubt about my dad's involvement that night. He wasn't driving. I've had a glimpse of the old him, and I want him back. We need to do whatever we can to make this right now. If that means watching him and Bradbury like hawks then so be it. Bradbury's a bully. He'll slip up sooner or later. They always do.'

I nodded, but didn't share his optimism. Bradbury had got this far in life taking advantage of those around him, beating, robbing, scheming and thieving. That comeuppance hadn't arrived yet. Dougie smiled; it was half-hearted. Perhaps he was trying to show me that he was back on-topic, the two of us together again, united in the mission like Kirk and Spock. (Don't even go there – I am *so* obviously Kirk in this scenario.) Maybe he was trying to show me he was confident we were going to come out of this unscathed. Like I say, his optimism was far from contagious. It was blinder than a bat in a shoebox. One that was blindfolded. Bradbury was a *very bad man.* Dougie tried to change the subject. We went with him, happy to be momentarily moving on from the dark subject of my killer.

'Enough worrying about my dad,' said Dougie. 'That'll sort itself out, no doubt and no worries. What are we going to do about this old gimmer?' he said, directing his comment towards the Major.

'Old?' exclaimed the Major, turning his face and jutting out his jaw, skin shimmering with that ghostly blue light. 'Do I look old to you? Look at this profile, Sparky. If it weren't for that war I'd have been on the silver screen. I'm forever young. I got a face to break a thousand hearts.'

'Break a thousand farts, more like,' said Dougie. 'And that was never your real hair colour. Silver screen? Silver fox, I reckon.'

'Don't disrespect the hair, kid!'

'Good stuff that Kiwi boot polish. Gets a nice shine, eh?'

The airman shook his head and looked my way. 'He's dead to me.'

We laughed as one, the tension that had hung in the air having dissipated, blown away on a breeze of good humour. Bradbury seemed far from my friends' minds as they sparred with one another. I, however, was sadly unable to shake the villain's spectre from my thoughts.

'When I ask what we're going to do with you, let me further explain,' said Dougie. 'If you remember, there was the small issue of your old flame, Ruby.'

The Major smiled dreamily, no doubt recalling some profoundly beautiful moment with his true love.

'Either he remembers or that's ghostly gut-rot,' said Dougie. 'Possibly something to add to the *Rules of Ghosting*?'

'Seriously though,' I said. 'What do you want to do? Do you want us to deliver a message to her? Dougie could let her know that he can reach you.'

The Major's smile slipped. 'What good would it do?'

That wasn't the reply I'd expected. 'The world of good, surely. You loved her, didn't you? And it's pretty flipping clear she loved you. Still does, for that matter.'

'How do you think she'll respond if Sparky tells her he can speak to me, that I'm still here?'

'She'll be overjoyed?'

'OK, kid. Try and imagine the effect a revelation like that would have on your dear old mom. Would she be thrilled?'

I imagined Mum's face as Dougie told her he could talk to my ghost. It wasn't a pretty image. The Major continued.

'She'll think it's a cruel prank. She'll be heartbroken.'

Dougie snapped his fingers, the light bulb moment sparking him into action. 'Then I tell Ruby something only you could know, something personal, just between the two of you.'

'Better, but still not great. Will's mom might be able to handle a shock like that, but Ruby? You said she's frail. News like that could do more damage than good. You going in there solo and blabbing about me could end in tears or worse. The message needs something physical alongside it, a token of proof that can ease her into the idea that I never went away. This is too big for you to go shooting your mouth off. Words aren't enough.'

'OK,' I said. 'Dougie's lack of tact taken into account, what would you suggest? Last time we chatted you mentioned something about the air base.'

'I did?'

'Yeah, but you were interrupted by Cornetto boy here.'

'I do love those ice creams,' said Dougie as I continued.

'Is there something there we could use?'

The Major scratched his jaw, as if the action of rubbing the chiselled chin would conjure an idea into life. It fairly worked.

'The mess,' he said.

'The what now?' asked Dougie.

'The old officers' mess.'

'What's that when it's at home?' Dougie said.

'It's where the officers lived, right?' I said, as the Major nodded.

'Lived, slept, ate and the rest. They were our digs while we were stationed here. We weren't with the boys in the barracks. We had a few luxuries, perks of station.'

'Perks?' said Dougie.

'We had our own bar, Sparky, a pool table, leather chairs, a gramophone—'

'Grandma's phone?'

The Major groaned. 'Gram-a-phone. You know, for long players? Vinyl records?'

Dougie stared at the Yank gormlessly.

'A music system,' I said, spelling it out for my hapless pal.

The Major nodded. 'Certainly made being far from home a bit more bearable for us.'

'What about this "mess" then?' said Dougie. 'What's so special about it?'

The American's face was serious, the cheeky grin departed as he leaned in close. 'So, downstairs was the day quarters where we socialised, but upstairs was where our cots were.'

'Beds!' said Dougie, with another fingersnap.

'Sharp as a tack, ain't he?' said the Major. 'My room was in the attic, highest room of the house.'

'Hang about,' I said. 'House? I thought you stayed in bunkers. Weren't you in one of those Anderson shelters, like we read about in History lessons?'

'We were officers, Will,' said the Major. 'They requisitioned a farmhouse for us on the land where the base was built. The farmer didn't object, taking a tidy sum off the Air Force and waving goodbye to the pigswill.'

'So there's something there that could help reunite you with Ruby?' asked Dougie.

'Reunite? Hell, no. The only way that could happen would be if she died, and I'm in no hurry for that to happen. I've waited long enough to see her. A little longer ain't gonna hurt. She clearly isn't done with your world yet, Sparky.'

'So what's the item?' I asked, cutting to the chase. 'And where is it?'

'Like I said, I was in the attic. We had a cast iron French stove up there that we used to warm the room and brew our coffee over. There was a round window at the gable end of the house that overlooked the base. My cot was beneath it, bed-head to the wall. I kept my valuables under the floorboards there, in a cigar box. Find the loose floorboard, you'll find the one thing that can convince Ruby this is all real, not the cruel prank of some teenage punks.'

'Valuables?'

'Yeah, kid. My cash, family keepsakes, love letters . . .'

Dougie and I nodded, understanding where our friend was heading.

'You want us to show Ruby the letters,' I said.

The Major shook his head. 'The letters are only part of it; there's something else in there as well.'

'Something else?' said Dougie, suddenly intrigued. 'Like what? Dirty pictures? Whisky? A gun?'

'Of course,' said the Yank in a mocking tone. 'All of that and more, Sparky! There's even a treasure map to a stash of stolen Nazi gold, buried on the banks of the ship canal. No, kid. No broads, booze or bullets I'm afraid. Just give her the box. Trust me, it'll make sense. That's all you need to do.'

'OK,' I said. 'So we find the cigar box and hand it over to Ruby?'

'Yeah,' said the Major, suddenly looking awkward. 'You don't need to open it though, understand? She can do that.'

'Understood.' I could tell that whatever he'd stored in that box was private. This was one of those rare occasions where there was no room for goofing about. Dougie nodded in silent agreement.

'There's one other thing, though,' I added.

'What's that?' said the Major.

'The air base isn't what it was.'

'Whaddaya mean?'

'They've started levelling it, remember? The newspaper article I showed you: they're knocking down the hangars, breaking up the runways and building houses over the lot.'

'What are you saying?'

'He's saying that finding your cigar box under the floorboards is the least of our worries,' said Dougie. 'We need to see if the farmhouse is still standing. It could have been demolished.'

'Demolished?' The Major punched a fist into his palm. 'I knew this was too good to be true. Nothing in life – or death – is ever simple.'

'Let's not get ahead of ourselves, Yank,' said Dougie, patting his hand through our friend's insubstantial back. 'First things first, eh? Let's find that farmhouse.'

EIGHTEEN

Bases and Boxes

'How are you getting on?' I whispered into Dougie's ear as he snipped the last length of mesh with his wire cutters. He jumped at my voice.

'You've an uncanny knack for the heebiejeebies, y'know?'

'Sorry.'

'If it's not your voice coming out of nowhere, it's your ugly face looming over me every morning,' Dougie said, dropping the wire cutters back into his messenger bag.

'I do that?'

'Yep. No respect for personal space. I'd say it's a ghost thing, but you were an idiot when you were alive too.'

Dougie took hold of the wire fence. He carefully pulled it back in gloved hands before slipping through, gently allowing the severed mesh to fall back without rattling. The last thing we needed was to alert the security guards to Dougie's presence.

He looked the business, decked in his stealthiest subterfuge gear. Dougie was all too aware that this was a potentially dangerous task he was undertaking: 'ninja black' was the dress code he'd insisted upon. He stopped short of saying he may not return alive. Admittedly the effect of his outfit was lessened somewhat by the *Iron Maiden* T-shirt, but all things considered it was a fair effort. Furthermore, my knowledge of ninjas was admittedly limited, but I doubted they usually took man-bags on missions with them, Dougie's messenger bag bouncing jauntily upon his hip.

'We need to cut across this field,' I said, indicating straight ahead with my hand. 'Mind your step, though. The barracks used to be situated across this meadow. Goodness knows what's underfoot.'

Knowing what the plan was, we'd wasted no time in scouring the internet for information on the air base. Photos and plans of the site had been examined, the farmhouse located, and the quickest, safest route to it decided. The enormous shadow of an aircraft hangar loomed large nearby.

'According to the maps, the farmhouse is at the back of that hangar. Just need to watch out for the security patrols.'

Right on cue, a beam of torchlight flashed close by to our

right, an approaching guard doing his rounds of the perimeter fence.

'You might want to move,' I said, but my pal needed no prompting. He was off, staying low to the long grass. I sped after him, pulled along by Dougie's invisible tether, my eyes never leaving the torch beam at our backs. He leapt suddenly, hurdling a crumbling low wall that had appeared out of nowhere from the weed-riddled field. There was a clanging as his feet hit something metallic, hidden in the grass. He cursed aloud as his trainers went from under him, the uneven surface sending him sprawling through the air.

Dougie hit the dirt and spluttered as I hovered over him. Back the way we'd come I caught sight of the guard's torch sweeping the darkness in our direction. Had he heard our din? He'd need to be deaf to have missed it. I crouched beside Dougie.

'You OK?' I asked. He winced.

'My ankle. Think I might've sprained it.'

'Can you walk on it?'

'I'm going to have to, aren't I?'

He set off, stumbling through the grass and drawing nearer the hangar. Behind us, the torch cut through the night, closing in, searching for the cause of the commotion.

'Come on, D,' I said, urging him on. 'Imagine you've got a pack of zombies at your back. Better still, imagine it's Vinnie Savage and his cronies!'

That did the trick. Dougie found an extra gear, opening his stride as he loped painfully toward the hangar. Soon we were slipping into its towering shadow, my friend hugging its wall breathlessly as I scouted our surroundings.

'We've shaken the security guard, mate, for now. But we need to keep moving.'

Dougie nodded, his face contorting like he might barf. Then he was moving again, hobbling along the edge of the aircraft hanger, making his way to the rear. I looked up as we went, overwhelmed by the sheer scale of the thing. This was the last giant standing, the others long gone, just like the Major and his old comrades. Only ghosts remained.

We slowly turned the corner of the hangar, searching for guards and, more importantly, a farmhouse. I hadn't expected it to still be standing. Surely that would've been the first thing to go, a clapped-out, crumbling building. Yet there it was, a ruin rising from the wasteland, bedecked in rubble. Dougie wasted no more time, skipping clumsily across broken tarmac to the farmhouse, wincing as he went.

The front door hung open crazily, the timber green with lichen. Dougie squeezed through the gap, blinking as his eyes adjusted to the gloom.

'It's like a giant dumpster,' I said.

Once home to Air Force officers, the ground floor had gone through a makeover. The building had been used as a landfill in recent years, a dumping ground for all manner of debris. Bricks, bags of mortar and busted construction materials cluttered one wall, while more residential waste filled the remainder of the large room. A knackered toilet sat beside the staircase, its porcelain cracked and riddled with mould. Bin bags were piled high in one corner, the buzz of flies and Dougie's contorting nostrils telling me something nasty was within. Pizza boxes, crumpled cans and broken bottles were a popular decoration, popping up all over the place. An ancient-looking television set stood proud in the room's centre, its screen smashed, audience long departed.

'Upstairs,' I said, and Dougie was off, struggling up the creaking staircase as he made for the next floor. The landing was cluttered with more junk but we pressed on through, swinging around to find the attic steps. Up he went, the rotten, twisted timbers groaning beneath his weight. I held my breath for Dougie, hoping the staircase would hold out and not plunge him into the chaos below. Finally, he reached the summit.

'He lived here?' whispered Dougie.

'Suspect it was more homely back in the day,' I said.

Half the ceiling was missing, revealing jagged joists, shattered roof-tiles cluttering the ground where they'd landed down the years. Great holes pockmarked the floor where the exposed wood had been worn away by the weather, eventually falling through to the rooms below. There was the rusting French stove, balanced precariously beside one such hole, suicidal on its fragile perch. Only the occasional beam remained. Dougie stepped forward, jumping with fright as half a dozen crows took flight from the shadows, disappearing through the splintered roof.

'The round window,' I said, pointing ahead across the dangerous ground. There it was, in the centre of the gable-end wall, the only sheet of glass still intact in the farmhouse as far as we could tell.

'It would have to be on the far side of the attic, wouldn't it?' grumbled Dougie.

'Can't make it too easy for you.'

Dougie inched forward across the beams, slipping occasionally on bird poop that had been kindly deposited upon the mulchy timber. His arms remained out on either side of him, body lurching occasionally as he battled for balance. I'd seen better tightrope walkers at the circus, but none so brave as my mate as he struggled on, effectively on one leg. I drifted beside him, unhindered by earthly restrictions, floating freely across the air.

'There!' I said, jabbing a finger ahead and instantly regretting it.

Dougie jumped with alarm. His body twisted as he tried to remain upright. It was no good. His bad foot went out from under him, causing him to spin round. Both feet flew out to the sides, causing him to land astride the beam with a groin-crunching thud. The French stove fell, crashing into the darkness below. Dougie didn't have time to hurl, instead sliding off the timber and into space. It was only the messenger bag that saved him; the handle caught a jagged outcropping of wood that had once been a joist, leaving him dangling in mid-air, halfway between two floors. He recovered his senses, clutching his man-bag and looking to me in a justifiably exasperated fashion.

'Sorry,' I whispered. 'I can see it though, dead ahead!'

Dougie squinted and followed my pointing finger. There it was, the unmistakable sight of a cigar box, jutting precariously from the wall between broken boards. Dougie groaned, his forearms looped through his strap, hopeless and helpless, so close to our prize. The spur of wood he was suspended from looked like it might give at any moment, plunging him to the floor below. 'I'm kind of preoccupied,' he grunted.

A noise below caused us both to start; the front door was creaking open. Even from the attic we could see the torch's beam flickering through the crumbling building below.

'Who's there?' A gruff, angry voice.

'He doesn't sound happy,' I said.

'Deep joy,' whispered Dougie, forehead glistening with sweat as he began to slip through the loop of his messenger bag.

I looked back to the cigar box where it sat proud of the broken attic floorboards. I drifted across, our umbilical connection humming as I went. It was a strange sensation; the air charged with electricity the further we moved apart. Even in ghostly form I felt my skin prickle, hair standing on end, and I knew Dougie felt the exact same way. I hovered over the box, my heart like a jackhammer, so close to what we were searching for. I heard the guard's footsteps on the stairs as he began to climb, boards straining loudly beneath his feet.

'Can you grab it?' Dougie grunted, shoulders almost dislocated as he continued to slip free, strap edging closer to coming free from the joist.

'I heard that, you little sods!' called the security guard, catching Dougie's question. 'You're in a world of trouble!' His footsteps were swift now as he rushed up the flights.

I snatched at the box, but my hand went clean through, failing to connect. I closed my eyes, focusing for a moment, channelling my emotions and energies into my hands. I reached back slowly, hooking my palms behind the cigar box, and took a breath.

It all happened at once.

The guard arrived at the attic landing, cast his torch beam across the room. It lit Dougie's face up like a jack-o-lantern. Dougie panicked, his strap tore free from the splintered joist, and he plummeted. I was yanked away, our connection as tight as a rope about my waist. My fingers snatched at the box before I was hurtling down through the farmhouse after my friend. Dougie crashed through the rotten timbers of the first floor before hitting the pile of stinking bin bags. As I arrived beside him, so did the cigar box, landing in his lap, covered in a light coating of fresh ectoplasm.

'Sorry about that,' I muttered as he wiped the spooky jelly from his hands and shoved the box in his messenger bag.

'No time for gassing,' he said, rolling off the rubbish sacks and scrambling for the exit. We were out the door, cutting across the tarmac and past the corner of the aircraft hangar. Behind, we heard the security guard shouting as he gave chase.

'Which way?' cried Dougie, his bearings lost in the heat of the moment, his body pushed to its limits.

'That way,' I said, giving him a shove and connecting, buffeting him in the direction of the ruined barracks.

The torch light illuminated the grass around us now as we ran, accompanied by others as more guards joined the pursuit. Dougie was sobbing now, terror driving him on, fear of what the men might do should they catch him. I shared that horror as the shouting of the guards drew closer. He hopped and fumbled his way through the ruined buildings once more, this time grazing a shin on a sheet of rusted corrugated metal. His jeans tore along with the skin, causing him to cry out in pain. He went down, landing on all fours, struggling for breath. The messenger bag spilled open, wire cutters, can of Coke, Mars bar and cigar box all tumbling into the dirt.

'Get up!' I screamed at him, begging him to move, but at that moment he was done. I looked back as three torch beams converged upon the old barracks. Was this it? Only now did I realise the world of trouble my friend would be in if he was caught. School, the police, his future, his dad, the Major . . .

Dougie looked up, his panting ceasing, his face agog. I followed his gaze toward the cigar box.

The box radiated a pale blue light, growing brighter by the second until it shone brilliant and white. Shapes materialised around us, thin glowing slivers breaking free of the darkness. They coalesced before our eyes, stepping through the rubble, taking shape slowly. The one closest shifted into the form of a military man, not unlike the Major. His body was made of the same ethereal mist, translucent and spectral, the approaching security men visible through his form. He said nothing, saluting us once before turning toward the approaching guards, his companion ghosts gathering around him. They blinked out of existence as the atmosphere changed, the warm summer evening transformed in a heartbeat.

The wind blew up out of nowhere, swirling around and through the ruined barracks like a dust devil, tearing up grass and whipping it through the air. Dougie and I were in the eye of the storm; the guards suddenly ceased their advance, throwing their hands up before them. Dry earth took flight, caught on the tiny twister's thermals as the wind changed direction. It was sudden and savage, directed hard and fast at the security men, knocking them off their feet and sending them stumbling away.

I shouted at Dougie over the roar of the storm. Whether he heard me or not, he was up and moving again, snatching up the cigar box as we covered the remaining distance to the fence.

'What the hell was that?' I gasped, as Dougie squeezed through the severed mesh.

'Run,' he said. 'Just run.'

We dashed into the darkness, the panicked cries of the guards chasing us through the night.

NINETEEN

Errands and Errors

'Where are we going again?' asked Lucy, fingers entwined in Dougie's, the sun blazing overhead.

'It's just an errand, for my dad,' said a limping Dougie, the cigar box tucked into his waistband out of sight. 'He wants me to drop something off for a friend.'

Lucy nodded, seemingly satisfied with his explanation. We were walking through a neighbourhood he and I had only recently visited. Houses gave way to bungalows as we passed through an oasis of sheltered homes for the elderly. My eyes were drawn to the gardens. Many were well kept; lawns freshly mowed, shrubs manicured, rose bushes in bloom. Loved ones had clearly called by, taking care of these tasks for their infirm relatives. But what of those gardens that were jungles, overgrown by weeds and ivy. Where were their loved ones? These gardens were forgotten and unloved, as were those who hid behind the closed doors.

I sighed, and Dougie heard it. He caught me looking. Maybe he felt the same way. Perhaps I had a unique perspective, having passed over. Well, almost passed over, anyway.

'So your leg; what's with the limp?'

Dougie managed a smile as he hobbled along. 'Oh, this? Just an accident. I was playing football. No big deal.'

'You playing football?' I laughed as I shadowed them. 'Your encounter with a platoon of ghosts was more believable!'

He smiled and ignored me, and Lucy didn't doubt him. She rested her head on his shoulder as they walked on. I had to admit it: they made a great couple. They were hardly boyfriend-girlfriend material, looking in from the outside, but something had drawn them together. He was a big old geek, just like me, sharing the same oddball sense of humour. Not for the first time I was left wondering if things could have turned out differently if Bradbury hadn't got behind the wheel of Mr Hancock's Bentley. I shook my head and decided to let it go. These things could eat away at you. I never wanted to be in that situation again. I was happy for my pal, and he was happy with Lucy. The hot, foxy, drop-dead gorgeous Lucy who I'd fancied like mad throughout high school. Yeah, let's just say that their relationship was a work in progress for me and leave it at that, eh?

'Is something the matter, Dougie?' she asked.

'What do you mean?'

'With us? You've seemed . . . distant. Preoccupied.'

'Oh. There's just stuff going on at home, with my dad. Family stuff. I wouldn't want to bore you.'

'It wouldn't be boring, Dougie. You could tell me anything. If something's bothering you, please know I'm here for you.'

'Word to the wise,' I whispered. 'Probably not a good idea to mention me. Last time you did she conveniently blanked it from her memory, like it never happened. I'd stick with the family alibi if I were you.'

'Yeah,' said Dougie, answering the both of us. 'It's just family stuff. Please don't worry.' He kissed her. 'I'm fine, just a bit stressed out with stuff my dad's going through.'

She looked up. 'You *can* tell me, you know?'

Dougie stared into her eyes. I could see from his goofy expression what he was thinking.

'Don't spill your beans, pal.'

'My dad . . . is in a bit of a fix.'

I rolled my eyes. 'Mate, if this doesn't send her running, nothing will.'

He continued, regardless. 'He's been pretty low lately, not well at all. It's all on account of this guy he used to work for.'

'Used to? Is he no longer working?'

Dougie shrugged. 'It's difficult. He's been off work sick for a while now, but this guy wants him to do another job for him. Only I don't want him to do it.'

'Why?'

'His boss is a bad bloke. Very bad.'

'Sounds ominous,' she said quietly.

'You don't know the half of it. He makes Vinnie Savage look like Mickey Mouse.'

'So why doesn't your dad just tell him "no", then? Nobody can be *made* to work for someone. There are laws against that rubbish.'

'It isn't as simple as that. Dad's being blackmailed.'

'Blackmailed? With what?'

'I can't tell you,' said Dougie, his voice cracking with emotion and relief to at least be partially coming clean with Lucy. 'But it's something awful, trust me. I honest to God can't tell you, Lucy, you have to believe me!'

'I do believe you,' she said, squeezing his hand earnestly. 'Then surely he should go to the police and report this man?'

'No, he really can't. What Dad's implicated in . . .' He glanced at me, fleetingly. 'It's about as bad as it gets. And it's all untrue,' he added, aware that he might be painting Mr Hancock as a villain too.

The two of them walked on in silence. I strode beside my pal, sucking my teeth.

'Well. This is awkward. I *did* tell you not to tell her.'

Before he could answer, Lucy spoke up. 'I'm here for you, Dougie. And when you're ready to tell me what's really gone on, you will. Believe me, I can be more use to you if you tell me the whole truth, not snippets. Friends shouldn't keep secrets from one another.'

There was that word again: secrets. The Major had told me never to hide things from my friend, and here was Lucy using the exact same phrase. Coming clean with Dougie had hardly been a great idea at the time, resulting in a punch-up and prolonged period of ignoring one another. Would my friend face the same fate if he told Lucy what had happened? Before I could warn him, we were coming to a slow, staggered halt outside Ruby Hershey's bungalow. My heart sank.

The crowd were gathered around the back doors of the ambulance, the lights flashing on its roof, the siren silent. Most of the folk were neighbours, elderly friends who had been drawn out of their homes by the commotion. Many shared the same worried expressions on their faces, the odd one unreadable, showing little emotion. Perhaps they'd seen this sad scene occur once too often?

Dougie pushed through the crowd as politely as possible, leaving Lucy behind. I went with him, passing through the pensioners to the front in time to see the doors slam shut. I continued on, stepping through the back of the ambulance and materialising within. A paramedic crouched beside a trolley, checking a drip feed. The man spoke through the partition to his companions in the cab, relaying information about his patient's condition, but I didn't hear a word of it. My eyes were drawn to the old lady, motionless beneath the blankets, only her head poking out of the top. There was an oxygen mask over her mouth and nose, misting as her frail breath came out in ragged, reed-thin rasps. Her eyes fluttered. For an instant I thought she saw me, lids widening before slowly closing. The engine fired and the sirens wailed into life. The ambulance was moving then, drawing away, leaving me standing in the road as it drove off.

The crowd was already dispersing, only Dougie and Lucy remaining in the street. My friend's face was ashen. Unable to speak to me in his girlfriend's presence, he simply flexed his shoulders, looking to me for answers.

'She's alive.' I didn't know any more than that. In answer to our concerns we heard the bungalow front door slam shut. We looked over the fence and spied Ruby's nurse locking up. The squat lady made her way up the overgrown path, medicine case under one arm, paperwork in the other. She looked up when she reached the gate, recognising Dougie instantly.

'Mrs Hershey's great-grandson, right?' she said sadly. She shoved her papers into the crook of her one arm and then threw the other around Dougie, pulling him close until his face hit her blue-uniformed bosom. 'You poor love. What a terrible thing to happen to your great-gran, eh?'

Dougie prised himself free, taking an awkward step clear. 'What happened?'

'She had a funny turn, bless her. Probably this awful blooming heatwave we're having. She had no windows open.'

'Perhaps she was afraid?' offered Lucy, trying to catch up on the conversation and quite out of the loop. 'You know, of break-ins?'

The nurse looked her up and down as she stepped past toward her car, opening the boot. 'Perhaps, lovely,' she replied as she deposited her gear into the car. 'Did you know his great-gran too?'

'Gran—?' began Lucy, before Dougie jumped in.

'Where are they taking her, Miss?'

'The General Hospital. You should really let your parents know as soon as possible.' She pulled a mobile phone from her pocket. 'Do you want to call them? They live local, right?'

Dougie's smile was sad and very real. 'Thanks, but I'm going to head straight home now and tell them. You've already been too kind.'

'I'll see you down there,' said the nurse, opening the driver's door. 'Can give you a lift, if you like?'

'Thanks, but no thanks,' said Dougie, already backing away,

taking Lucy by the hand. 'I'd best check in with my folks first though.'

'Alright, petal,' she said. 'I'll see you down there. God bless.'

With that, she was in her car gunning the engine, as Dougie and Lucy walked in the opposite direction.

'What was she on about?' asked Lucy, her brow furrowed with suspicion. 'I didn't follow half of that. I thought your grandparents were all dead? You've never once mentioned a great-grandma. Also, since when did you have parents, plural? What was all that about?'

Dougie had no answers. His mouth opened, jaw moving, but no sounds came out.

'Say something, dude,' I said, all too aware he was drowning as Lucy's anger grew.

The plan had been straightforward enough. He was going to just pop in and drop the cigar box off with Ruby, tell her it was from a friend. That should have been all. He hadn't even intended to hang around. Taking along Lucy shouldn't have been a big deal – she would wait in the street – yet here we were once more, fate kicking us in the down-belows.

'Well?' she said, pulling her hand free from his. Any compassion she'd felt earlier was gone, replaced by irritation. 'That old woman *wasn't* your great-gran, was she? I'm not stupid. You must think I was born yesterday. Keeping stuff about your dad from me, I can just about handle. I'm all too aware that you've not introduced me to him yet which, let's face it, is a bit sodding weird. But this? Have you really nothing to say? You've just stood there and lied to that nurse. You're lying to me now. *Speak*, Dougie. What's going on?'

'Shout!' I said. 'Sing. Dance. Say *something*, mate!'

But Dougie simply stood there, shell-shocked, bereft of any answers that might appease Lucy.

'Fine,' she said haughtily. She unsnapped the silver charm bracelet from her wrist and slapped it into his hand. 'You can keep that. When you want to be honest – and I mean *truly* honest – we can see if that bracelet still fits. Until then you can keep it. Better still, give it to Great-Gran, whoever she is.'

Lucy stormed down the street without looking back. We watched her go. I could tell by her shaking shoulders she was crying.

'Mate,' I said, managing a pat of commiseration on his shoulder. 'You've still got me.'

The look he shot me could best be described as death warmed up. He pocketed the charm bracelet and clapped his hands together, just the once.

'Winner,' sighed Dougie miserably.

TWENTY

Listen and Learn

The journey back to Casa Hancock was less than enjoyable. I tried chatting to Dougie, but it was no good; he had one on him. A cloud hung over his head, peeing on his parade and dogging every sodden step. That business with Lucy had put a massive dampener on his demeanour, transforming him into the mean and moody Dougie who rarely came out to play. What few words escaped his mouth were curses, some directed at me, most directed at his misfortune. He managed to boot many objects en route: fences, lampposts, cans, his heels and even a luckless bee that got in his way. That backfired, of course, the insect pursuing him down the road for a good forty yards as he fled in abject fear. Mean and moody he may have appeared, but he was still my scaredy-cat mate on the inside.

We marched down his cul-de-sac, turning into his drive and

trooping around the side of the house. Dougie let himself in the back door, through to the kitchen, and I followed. He was about to dump his keys on to the sideboard when he stopped; we could both hear his father talking in the other room.

'Who's in there?' I asked.

'Dunno. He hasn't had a visitor for months.'

Judging by Mr Hancock's voice, he wasn't happy, his stressed tone hinting at an uncomfortable conversation.

'Hang about,' I said. 'It's just his voice. He's on the phone again.'

It wasn't like he ever spoke on the phone either. I could tell what Dougie was thinking: Bradbury. My friend was looking at the telephone extension that hung from the wall beside the bread bin. I could see him chewing his lip, considering what to do. His anxiety passed over to me, flooding me with a sickly, nervous energy. He was suddenly reaching for the receiver, fingers trembling.

I flung my hand out, the action enough to jar the progress of his hand and send it towards the bread bin.

'What?' he hissed.

'He might hear you pick up. That "click" that tells you someone's on the line; is that what you want? He'll be down on you like a ton of bricks if he catches you earwigging.'

'I need to know what's being said. If it *is* Bradbury, I can't have Dad working for him again, Will.'

'Then let *me* do the eavesdropping,' I said. 'Get over to the wall and I'll do the rest.'

Dougie crept across the kitchen to the dining area, slipping up to the wall. I gave him a confident wink, but I wasn't feeling it. The more time I spent in close proximity to Mr Hancock, the more I suspected he was becoming aware of my presence. It was inexplicable, just a terrible hunch I might get rumbled at any moment. He was there that night, after all. He was involved, whether he liked it or not.

I phased through the wall and into the lounge. Mr Hancock was sat in his trusty armchair, bent double, receiver in hand. His body language wasn't good. Furtive glances toward the glass door told me he was ashamed, fearful of Dougie's return, perhaps discovering what he was up to.

'I got that,' he said. 'But who am I driving?'

I darted forward, bringing my face up close to Mr Hancock's with such sudden velocity that I nearly ended up inside his head. I've done that once before with Dougie – just the once, mind you. As a ghost, there's nothing guaranteed to make you want to blow chunks more than materialising in a living person's head! I stopped an inch short of the man's skull and listened in to the telephone earpiece.

'You don't know the boys,' said the voice on the other end. The Liverpudlian accent was instantly recognisable.

'I might not know them, but I want names. I won't let just anyone in the Bentley.'

'Chill out, George,' said Bradbury. 'Don't get arsey. It'll be me and three of my best lads on this, all good boys. In and out, quick as a flash. Bish, bosh, bash; job done. I swear, this'll be the easiest gig in the world. Like taking candy from a baby.'

'Then I'm done?'

'Then we're done, George. I wouldn't be asking you to do this if it weren't an emergency. You know that.'

I caught Mr Hancock's sneer. It was clear he suspected otherwise, and so did we. Bradbury was toying with him, seeing how many hoops the poor chap would jump through. And to what end? To prove he had power over him. There was no way this would be the last phone call. This job was the thin end of the wedge. More work would follow, as would the threats.

'What time tonight?'

'Get there for two. Park in the loading bay. You need to be there prompt, not a minute later. Everyone will know where to find you.'

'Two o'clock?'

'What? Are you deaf now?' There was the aggression in Bradbury's voice, his mask slipping. His voice softened quick as a flash. 'Yeah, two. That alright, George?'

Mr Hancock grunted into the mouthpiece.

'I need to hear you say it,' said the man, his quiet voice dripping with menace. 'Yes, Mr Bradbury. Two o'clock.'

Dougie's dad shuddered. 'Yes, Mr Bradbury. Two o'clock, sir.'

'Sir. I like that. A real ring of respect to it. We're nothing without manners, eh, mate? Funny thing is, I've got you to thank for this job.'

'I don't follow.'

'Your lad gave me the idea when I met him the other day.'

Mr Hancock's jaw clenched suddenly. I saw his nose curl, like he'd caught the whiff of something rotten. He ground his teeth.

'My son gave you the idea?'

'Indirectly, George,' laughed Bradbury. 'I don't want you think I'm taking him on as an apprentice or 'owt. He won't be aware he helped me. No, the idea came from bumping into him.'

I watched Dougie's dad exhale slowly, trying to keep his composure in the face of the villain's words. 'Is that all?'

'That's all, George. I'll see you later, eh?'

'This is the last one, remember?'

'Oh aye,' chuckled Bradbury. 'Of course it is.'

The phone went dead in Dougie's father's hand. I backed up as Mr Hancock smacked his parched lips. His hand went instinctively to a beer can at the foot of the armchair, wavering for a moment. He snapped it back, thinking better of it. At that moment I spied an open notepad on his thigh, pencil notes scrawled on the top sheet. Before I could read it, he was tearing the leaf off, folding it and tucking it into his shirt breast pocket. I cursed my ill timing as he rose, pad and pencil falling off his lap to the debris-littered carpet.

'Oh, hello,' he said, taken aback. He was looking straight at me!

I gasped.

I was about to reply when I heard Dougie's voice at my back. He was standing in the open hall doorway.

'Everything OK, Dad?'

'Yes, Douglas,' he said, cheeks flushed with colour, and it wasn't the booze. He was shamefaced to be lying brazenly to his son. 'All good.'

'What're you up to? Were you on the phone?'

'Yeah, just a nuisance call. Some idiots trying to sell us stuff. What are they like, eh?'

Mr Hancock made to move past Dougie, but my pal remained blocking the door.

'Is everything alright, Dad? Really?'

His father's shoulders slumped. 'Everything *will* be alright, son. Trust me.'

With that, Dougie reluctantly stepped aside. Mr Hancock sloped into the kitchen, stopping at the internal door that led through to the garage. Keys jangled, the door opened, and he went through, locking it behind him. Dougie turned to me.

'What was that all about then?'

'He wasn't being entirely truthful.'

'Let's go with the word "remotely". I know my dad. What was said?'

I moved away from the door, encouraging Dougie to follow. The last thing he needed was for his dad to hear him confabbing with himself.

'He's doing a job for Bradbury,' I said.

'Why?' said Dougie, loudly, immediately cringing in case his father heard him. 'Why do *anything* for that scumbag?'

'I'm with you, mate. But look at the facts. Bradbury still has him over a barrel. There's no way he wants to do this, but he clearly feels he has to.'

'It's me, isn't it? Am I the bargaining chip? Is he using me as a threat?'

'I'm sure you're a major part of it, but let's not rule out the idea that Bradbury could also send some heavies round and kneecap your dad. He's seriously bad news. Your dad's terrified.'

Dougie shook his head bitterly. 'What's the job?'

'Don't know, I only caught the tail end of the conversation, but it's happening at two o'clock tonight.'

'Tonight?'

'Bradbury reckons *you* gave him the idea for it.'

'Me?'

'I know. Proper little Moriarty and you don't even know it.'

'So what's the job?'

'He wrote down the details on his notepad – but mate, I'm so sorry. He tore the sheet off and took it with him.'

'Where did he put the note?'

'Shirt pocket. With respect to your old man, he's been sleeping in that shirt all week. I don't think you've got a hope in hell of picking that pocket.'

Dougie cursed and kicked an empty beer can across the floor. His eyes flashed as he spied something. Crouching, he picked it up. He waved the notepad at me.

'This pad?'

I nodded, as my mate snatched up the pencil. He turned it on its side and began to run it back and forth lightly against the top sheet of the pad, carefully increasing the pressure. It was as if he were doing a brass rubbing which his life depended upon. Gradually the words materialised through the shades of graphite, the indentations left behind on the pad from Mr Hancock's writing slowly revealing themselves. We brought our faces in close. There were the road names accompanied by a crudely sketched map.

'It's in town, look,' I said, pointing out Buttermarket Street in Dougie's dad's scrawl. There was the loading bay Bradbury had mentioned too, circled roughly with a 'C' for car. Dougie jabbed at a point on the rough map that had a big cross on it.

'X marks the spot.'

'What *is* that building?' I asked. I could see it was on a pedestrianised part of the street. Dougie gulped with realisation, tapping the sketch with a forefinger.

'That's the alley Vinnie Savage chased us into. It's where Bradbury met us.'

'That alley?' I remembered it only too well now, including its location. 'Bloody hell, Dougie. You know what this is, don't you?'

'Yes,' said my frightened friend. We both heard the Bentley rev into life for the first time since forever.

'It's a bank job.'

TWENTY-ONE

Schemes and Dreams

There are some things in life one should never underestimate. The unstoppable, vengeful fury of an enraged older brother would be one such thing, especially if you've just kicked him up the arse. The never-ending cost upon your well-being and safety when dating the school bully's ex-girlfriend would be another. And the ability for Stu Singer to steal every item off your still-warm corpse during a game of *Dungeons & Dragons* would always rank pretty high. The love a father has for his son would be in the top three too. That's a pretty special bond and a powerful set of emotions we're looking at there. Likewise, it swings both ways. There's little a son wouldn't do for his father.

Amongst the many things that united Dougie and I throughout our lives – and my death, let's not forget – was our love of literature. We shared a deep-rooted obsession with roleplaying games, comics, films and music, but it was our fondness of a good book that really sealed the deal in the best mate stakes. If he'd read it, chances were so had I. One of our favourite authors we had discovered in primary school: Roald Dahl. But that great writer divided our opinion. What was the master storyteller's greatest book? We were agreed that, unusually, it wasn't one of his more fantastic works. Charlie, the Twits and Mr Fox had their place of course, but they weren't our favourites. Mine was *Tales of the Unexpected*, my own father having introduced me to them when I was little, even showing me to the old TV show that was broadcast when he was in short pants. I loved a good short story, especially one with a twist, and *Tales* was full of them. However, Dougie's favourite struck a chord far closer to home.

My friend loved *Danny, Champion of the World*. No friendly giants, no glass elevators, no marvellous medicines. It was a very real story about a boy and his father, two friends who would do anything for one another. In Dougie's words, it was the most wonderful, perfect example of a father-son relationship in literature. I found it hard to argue. Perhaps this was the dream for Dougie, to have that exact same bond with his old man. One could hardly blame him. Whenever the subject arose I found myself having to re-evaluate my love for *Tales*.

And it was *Danny* that would inspire Dougie as he sought to save his own father from a terrible fate.

That evening, while Mr Hancock tinkered with the Bentley, preparing for the job, Dougie went through his usual routine. He washed up the pots and pans from the previous night and prepared dinner for the coming one. Dinner in Casa Hancock wasn't terribly thrilling or healthy for that matter. Sausage and bacon butties were the norm with Dougie on chef duty, and the closest one came to the five-a-day portions of fruit and veg was tomato ketchup. On this particular evening, beans and toast were on the menu. However, a secret ingredient had been added to the dish, one that would hopefully scupper Mr Hancock's involvement in Bradbury's scheme.

Dougie's dad came through from the garage, closing and locking the door behind him. His hands were filthy, caked in dirt and grime after spending the last few hours working on his car. He whacked the tap with his elbow, a torrent of water streaming over his hands.

'What's the occasion?' asked Dougie, stirring the beans. 'You haven't taken the car out for ages.'

Mr Hancock didn't answer, instead scrubbing his fingers with a soapy nailbrush.

'I know what you're up to, Dad, and I still say you're daft.' This was his last chance to reason with him. 'Tell Bradbury to go whistle.'

Mr Hancock stopped cleaning, letting the hot water wash away the suds. 'Son, there are some things we have to do in life which are unpleasant. But we do them, nonetheless. Let's leave it at that, eh?'

'You don't have to do anything you don't want to,' muttered my pal as four slices of toast popped from the machine. He snatched them up, whacking them on to a pair of plates and daubing them with butter.

'That's where you're wrong, Douglas. There are consequences to every action *and* inaction. If I don't do this one last thing for that man, he'll do something far more terrible than you can possibly imagine. Trust me, son. Ask no more questions. I do one last job for Bradbury and then he's out of our lives for good. You and I can move on. Together. Like it used to be.'

'You'll never be able to move on, Dad,' said Dougie, slopping the beans on to Mr Hancock's slices of toast. 'As long as he's out there, Bradbury owns you.'

His dad shook his head, not wanting to hear it. He picked up his dinner and cutlery from the work surface. Then he was gone, back into the lounge to eat his meal on his lap. Dougie and I stared at the mottled glass door. We could hear the television set, but above that the noise of his father's knife and fork scraping against the plate as he cut up and devoured his beans on toast. Dougie looked anxious.

'You not eating?' I asked.

'Strangely, I'm not in the mood for beans,' he replied, picking up a piece of toast from his plate and munching on the buttery slice. 'Do you think it'll work?'

'We'll have to wait and see,' I said, drifting across the room to take a peek into the lounge. Mr Hancock was already on to slice number two, chasing the beans around the plate, eyes fixed on the television. I returned to my pal.

'Seems your dad's got an appetite on him.'

'So now what?'

'We wait.'

Dougie tossed the half-eaten slice of toast back on to his plate. He looked like he might chunder at any moment. He pulled a stool out from the breakfast counter and slumped into it.

'What's the matter?'

'I hope we've done the right thing.'

'What option did you have?'

'I could've let him go and do the job.'

'And have that on your conscience, knowing you could've stopped him?' I shook my head. 'Don't be second guessing what you might have done.' I looked back towards the lounge. 'Besides, it's too late now.'

Dougie shivered. 'Will he be alright?'

I didn't know the answer so I went with the comforting lie

instead. 'I'm sure he'll be fine. You've done what anyone would do for a loved one. This is in his best interests.'

He looked at the phone on the wall.

'When should I call them?' he said.

'It's too soon. You need to wait for it to take effect. And besides, you weren't planning on using the landline, were you?'

'What? Should I use my mobile instead?'

'Sod that! You need to find a public phone-box.'

'Do they still even exist?'

I managed to smile. 'They certainly do. There's a museum piece outside St Mary's church you could use. But it has to be a public one. The *last* thing you need is to have the call traced back here. Then you and your dad would really have some explaining to do.'

Dougie nodded, seeing the bigger picture as I continued.

'Try not to worry. This time tomorrow, all your worries will be firmly behind you.'

Dougie winced where he sat, reaching down to gingerly rub his bad leg.

'Is that the one you injured on the air base?'

He pulled his left trouser leg up, rolling it back to his knee. I gagged when I saw the wound. A four-inch cut rode across his shin, the skin bulging and discoloured on either side of the ragged flesh. It wasn't scabbing over. I'd seen enough episodes of *Holby* to know an infection when I saw one.

'You *really* need to get that looked at.'

'I've cleaned it up. That'll have to do for now.'

'Dougie, I'm a ghost, but even *I* can smell how rank that is. Don't leave it any longer than you have to. Get down to A&E and have them stitch it up.'

My friend looked faint, like he might slide off the stool any second. 'I've got a thing about needles.'

'It's not the one with the thread you need to be worried about,' I chuckled mischievously. 'It's the tetanus jab in the butt that's *really* gonna hurt!'

'You're all heart, Underwood.' I caught him looking across the counter at the little brown medicine bottle. My laughter subsided.

'Let's give it an hour and see how he's doing,' I said. 'They should've kicked in by then.'

'That was double the prescribed number of pills,' said Dougie, chewing his lip anxiously. 'He's like Sleeping Beauty on the regular dose. We could be looking at Rip Van Winkle here.'

'Better Rip Van Winkle than the Prisoner of Azkaban! Come on. Let's go to your room, listen to tunes, kill the time. No good worrying now, mate.'

We left the kitchen, passing the lounge en route to the

stairs. We couldn't help but look through. Dougie's dad looked relaxed – *very* relaxed – in his armchair, the empty dinner plate on the floor at his feet.

'Sweet dreams, Mr Hancock,' I whispered as we left him to his approaching slumber and disappeared to Dougie's bedroom.

TWENTY-TWO

Done and Dusted

We were there when Mr Hancock finally stirred. He was in his armchair, exactly as he'd been left, still in his clothes from yesterday. That wasn't so unusual; the poor chap having taken slovenliness to new depths. He rubbed his eyes, smacked his lips and squinted at the sunlight that flooded the room. He seemed terribly confused, his gaze settling upon the television, unable to figure what was going on. Only the evening news had now been replaced by the morning news, and it told us a very different story.

'What . . . what happened?' he asked, hauling himself upright.

'What do you mean, Dad?' asked Dougie from the sofa. His father became agitated as he double-checked his wristwatch.

'How did I oversleep?' His voice was frantic. 'Why didn't you wake me?'

'Sorry,' said Dougie. 'Was there something important you had to do?'

Mr Hancock shook his head, unable to fathom his predicament.

'I don't understand . . . I just had a nap. How did I sleep right through? You *knew* I had somewhere to be, Douglas. And you let me sleep?'

'Let you? You had a job for Bradbury, Dad. Did you really think I'd stand by and watch you go ahead with it? After all that he's done? To you. Me. To Will?'

Mr Hancock struggled for a reply but was found wanting. I felt a warm glow at the mention of my name, but also a chill. Dougie had done right by me *and* his dad. His father wasn't seeing it, but his son's actions were completely justified. Hopefully he'd get with the programme shortly.

'You don't understand, Douglas,' said Mr Hancock fearfully, rising from the armchair. He seized the carriage clock from the mantelpiece, as if he might wake from a nightmare at any moment.

'What don't I understand, Dad?' Dougie shot up from the sofa so fast I thought he might head-butt the ceiling. 'Bradbury was using you. Again. Dragging you down into the gutter. You weren't going to haul yourself out, so it was left to me. You can thank me later.'

'He won't stand for this, Douglas! He's wicked. I was supposed to *be there* last night. I had a *job* to do!' He was panicking now, stepping towards Dougie, spittle flying.

'Back up, pal,' I said. 'He's lost it!'

Dougie ignored me, standing his ground as his father towered over him. I'd never seen Mr Hancock like this: equal parts terrified and terrifying. His hand went back, palm open.

'You stupid boy!'

Dougie remained there, unrepentant in the face of his father's ranting.

'You're going to hit me? For what? Saving your hide? It wasn't a job, Dad. Will's dad has a job. So does Stu's dad and Andy's. You never had a job. You worked for a criminal. I know *all about* what you were going to do last night. A bank robbery? Really? Is that all you are, some lowlife?'

Mr Hancock reeled back on his heels, backing away from his boy, besieged by shame. Anger gave way to grief.

'Why are you crying, Dad? We're shut of Bradbury now.'

'No we aren't, Douglas,' he sobbed. 'He was expecting me last night. Don't you see? He'll come after me!'

Dougie's laugh was short and sharp. 'You're not listening. Look at the telly. Please.'

His father turned slowly to the television. Realisation dawned on his face as the local newsreader reported the headline story.

'The four men who were captured last night during a foiled

bank robbery in Warrington are all known to the police. They are believed to be local criminals who have been operating across the Cheshire and Merseyside area. The men, believed to have been armed, were caught in the early hours in a carefully managed sting operation. Police say they are grateful to an anonymous tip that was received from a member of the public yesterday evening, alerting them to the failed heist. Anyone with further information on the attempted robbery is encouraged to contact Cheshire Constabulary or Crimestoppers.'

Mr Hancock looked at Dougie. 'You told the police?'

His son nodded, chest puffed out like a prize bantam. 'I did.'

'But what if the police had failed to capture them?'

'They didn't fail though, did they? They caught them. Four criminals, the newsreader said. It'll have been Bradbury and three others you were supposed to pick up. My maths has never been all that, but I'm pretty sure I'm on the ball with this one. They caught them, Dad. They have Bradbury.'

A smile flickered on his father's face. 'They have him?'

'You'd have to think so, wouldn't you? Armed too, the news said. That's got to come with a long stretch inside, surely?'

'And when they let him out?'

'*If* they let him out, right? You said he was wanted in connection with other crimes, no? Surely they'll throw the book at him.'

'But *if* they let him out . . .'

'Then we move. What's keeping us here?'

'I rather like it here,' I chimed in cheekily, but Dougie crashed on.

'It doesn't matter where we are, Dad, so long as we're together. Right? You used to say that, when I was little, before all this happened. We could be living in a hole in the ground and so long as we were together you'd be happy. That hasn't changed. We can be that happy again.'

'I just worry, son. What might happen to you, should Bradbury ever discover—'

'Please, stop worrying, Dad. It's over. It's done. Dusted. You're free. We can move on with our lives.'

Mr Hancock stood there, unsure of what to say, one hand clutching the mantel to keep steady.

'For God's sake, don't just stand there gawping at him,' I said. 'Go give your old man a hug!'

Dougie threw his arms around his father, Mr Hancock returning the embrace twofold. He lifted his son off the floor, Dougie's toes tapping at thin air as his dad squeezed with all his might. All his anger, shame and sorrow flooded out of him in that moment of pure and perfect love. The two of them wept freely while I shifted from one embarrassed foot to another. His dad might not have been able to see me, but Dougie certainly could. I felt like the king of all gooseberries so turned my back, affording them what privacy I could – no mean feat considering the spectral bungee. I watched the news instead, wondering what would become of Bradbury.

The monster who had killed me was off the streets at last and behind bars. I could see why Mr Hancock was anxious, but there was no way they'd let Bradbury walk free. He had a list of crimes as long as the Mersey, if the rumours were true. He'd be away for a long time. Things were looking up for the first time in ages. My mate and his dad were reunited. The beast was in chains . . . yet still, I felt a nagging concern about how it affected my predicament. Would I now move on at last, with justice done? Or was I cursed to hang around until Bradbury himself shuffled off the mortal coil? Did I need to pass the baton to him? How exactly did limbo work? The Major had given me no such answers; he was as clueless as me in that regard, in an equally rudderless boat. I was as lost as ever.

Dougie and his father pulled apart, each snorting back snotty tears. My mate jabbed his father in the chest.

'Here's an idea. Go take a shower. You smell rank.'

Mr Hancock laughed, sniffing his pits through the stained shirt. 'I suppose I do. Thanks, son.' He kissed him on the forehead. 'Love you.'

We watched him disappear upstairs, his trademark trudge replaced by a springing stride.

'Things are looking up,' I said. 'You must feel super chuffed. Everything's going your way.'

'Not everything,' he said, checking his mobile phone.

'What's the matter?'

'Lucy. I must've sent her a dozen texts, and she hasn't replied to one. Nothing. Not a sausage.'

'She'll come round, mate. With this Bradbury mess behind you now, perhaps you can start to enjoy life again. You may even be able to come completely clean with her too.'

'Completely?'

'If there's one thing we should've learned from recent shenanigans, surely it's that secrets are *very bad things.*'

'Hark at you with your sudden attack of morals.'

'It's as close as I come to telling cautionary tales. You and I, you and Lucy, you and your dad.'

'Hang about, I'm sensing a pattern emerging here!'

We both laughed.

'Honesty's the best policy, especially with your loved ones. Here endeth the lesson.'

Dougie whimpered as he pocketed his mobile into his jeans. He wobbled unsteadily.

'Right,' I said. 'Get get the cigar box and grab your keys. You've divved around enough. All roads lead to the hospital. You've got a date, pal.'

'I have?'

'Three, actually. Show the box to the Major, check in on Ruby and get stabbed in the bum by a needle.'

Dougie snatched up his keys from the mantelpiece. 'My day gets better. Howay then, Casper. Let's go.'

TWENTY-THREE

Chip and Ruby

'So you're Mrs Hershey's great-grandson, then?' said the ward sister, holding the door open for Dougie. 'The district nurse told us you'd be coming by. I'm sure your gran will be pleased to see you.'

Dougie limped into the geriatric ward, ears pricked at the good news. His messenger bag was slung over his shoulder, the cigar box safe inside. At no point in time had either of us contemplated opening it. We were quite often guilty of being impatient, impulsive teens but not on this occasion. The box was precious to the Major and whatever was hidden inside it was between him and Ruby Hershey.

'She's awake?'

The sister smiled as she led him down the corridor, past numerous shared rooms full of the elderly. 'Intermittently.

She's very poorly. There are moments of lucidity, but then she returns to a deep sleep. We're doing all we can to make her comfortable.'

'What happened, exactly?'

'Your gran suffered a cardiac event, probably exacerbated by the weather. As you can see, we're pretty much full to capacity here and many of the elderly have been coming in with heat-related illnesses. We're ensuring she has plenty of fluids and we're managing her pain relief.'

'Mate, this doesn't sound good,' I said as I drifted along beside Dougie, my eyes flitting through each side-ward in search of Ruby.

He and I had visited the hospital on countless occasions to meet with the Major, so much so that it had become like a second home, but geriatrics was one of the wards we hadn't visited before. There was something about the elderly that gave Dougie the shivers. Perhaps it was the inevitability of it all. Myself? I'd be forever young, to coin the Major's favourite saying, never growing old. Dougie was mortal, flesh and blood, and time waited for no man, not even my buddy. He had this to look forward to if he lived to a ripe old age.

Unlike Dougie, I experienced no such awkwardness here, in fact quite the opposite. I felt a closeness to the patients, a connection with them I hadn't experienced elsewhere in the hospital. Perhaps it was because many were so close to the end of the road. They weren't afraid of death. A good proportion would no doubt be welcoming it when the time came, their lives full, long years well spent. There was a colour to the geriatric ward that was missing from the others. Sunlight streamed in through every window, each room decked out with great bouquets of flowers. It was times like this that I missed my beating heart, envied the sense of smell which the living took for granted.

'Straight ahead,' said the sister, directing us toward a private room off the main ward. 'You're welcome to sit with her for a while. Visiting time ends in half an hour, lovely.' She smiled sweetly and went on her way, leaving us to enter the bedroom.

It was as if we'd stepped into another world, an altogether more solemn one at that. Ruby Hershey lay motionless in her bed, surrounded by a collection of medical paraphernalia. I recalled Stu's time in hospital after his fall from the Upper School roof. Those same pinging, blinking machines that he'd been hooked up to were now getting used on dear old Ruby. She looked a shadow of the woman we'd first met. Her cheeks were hollow, eye sockets dark, the misting of her face mask barely noticeable. There were no flowers on show, no stacks of get-well-soon cards, no shafts of daylight cutting through the gloom. This was a calm, quiet place. In that moment, I realised there was only one way Ruby was leaving the hospital. She was approaching the end.

The Major stood at the foot of her bed, his blue glow invisible to all but Dougie and I. I'd never seen him like this; he shone like a beacon, bright and beautiful, light rippling from him like waves from an aurora. He stood to attention, hands behind his back, keeping vigil over his love. He glanced our way as we approached, nodding solemnly before turning back to Ruby. The air was charged, death and desire, love and loss, swirling about us in a maelstrom. I looked down, my own palms throbbing with that same azure illumination, fingertips humming with an electric white fire. Was I feeding off the strange, heady atmosphere that came close to the moment of passing?

The Major spoke.

'I knew she was coming before she'd even arrived. I . . . sensed her. Knocked me sick, like a punch to the guts. By the time the ambulance pulled up I was on my knees.'

'We would've come sooner,' said Dougie. 'We wanted to tell you what had happened, at least warn you in advance, but something popped up. Stuff with my dad. And Bradbury.'

'It's alright, Sparky. I know how it is. These things are out of our hands. Life has a funny way of throwing curveballs. Besides, you couldn't have changed what had happened. Ruby would still be lying here, flitting in and out of consciousness.'

Dougie cleared his throat nervously. 'Is she . . . going to be OK?'

The Major smiled at the frail figure in the bed. 'Yes, Sparky, but not in the way you think.'

Dougie scratched his head, confused by the American's cryptic words, but I understood. The ghostly airman shared my certainty, a sense that Ruby wasn't long for this world. As if in an attempt to directly contradict our thoughts, the old lady stirred, turning her head on her pillow and releasing a soft moan. Dougie looked to the door, searching for the duty nurses as the Major dashed to Ruby's side. My friend was about to set off and call for help, when I reached out to grab him.

'The cigar box,' I said, snatching for his wrist.

It connected.

'What the—?' Dougie looked down to where my hand clutched his arm, eyes bulging with disbelief. I could feel his flesh within my hand, his skin against mine. Until this moment I'd forgotten that sensation, so real, so alive. It all came back in that split second, hitting me like a runaway bus. Every ounce of human contact I'd ever enjoyed – my parents, my brother, Dougie, Lucy. I kept hold, refusing to relinquish my grip, worried that if I did I might never feel that bond again.

'Bring the box, Dougie,' said the Major. 'Quickly!'

That was the one and only time I recall him ever using my friend's real name. It jolted Dougie into action, a lightning bolt to the brain. I let him go, my friend hopping to the bed on one leg and fishing the box from his bag. He gave it a quick polish with his T-shirt as the Major watched on, his expression caught between anticipation and anxiety. He fumbled with it, all too aware of the American's gaze upon him.

'Young man.'

Dougie almost dropped the box. Ruby's rheumy eyes had flickered open. They were fixed on my friend with a look of recognition.

'Mrs Hershey,' said Dougie, managing an awkward grin. He looked at the Major, who nodded with keen approval.

'Go on, Sparky. You can open it.'

'What do you have there, child?' asked Ruby, the mask misting as she spoke, obscuring her lips from view.

'It's a box of chocolates,' grinned Dougie, unable to resist joking as he fiddled with the latch.

'Chocolates? The ward sister *won't* be pleased. That's contraband!' She began laughing, but within seconds it had shifted into a fit of coughs.

'You stupid sod,' I said. 'You're going to give her another heart attack before you've opened the blooming box. Get on with it, you muppet!'

Ruby began to rise in the bed, the spluttering hacks threatening to fold her in two. The Major was there instantly, his hand upon her chest, connecting as surely as my own had moments ago with Dougie. The effect was instantaneous, relieving the old lady's painful attack. Gradually, Mrs Hershey eased back in her bed, comforted by that bright blue hand across her breastbone, slowly relaxing once more.

'The box,' whispered the Major without looking at us. Dougie's fingernails caught the little brass clasp and unhooked it, flipping the lid open.

I couldn't help but look. It reminded me of a time capsule, like the kind people buried beneath buildings. I remembered them doing something similar when I was in primary school and the new library was opened. The teachers wanted us to pick something thoughtful and worthy. Our class voted on what should go in there, each child trying to get their pick chosen. Thanks to democracy and bribery, that particular container – to be opened in years to come – would reveal an eclectic selection of treasures. The most notable item was a whoopee cushion that Stu Singer had campaigned for. This would be a warning to our descendants: never let children choose the contents of a time capsule.

The cigar box was a treasure trove from the Major's past. There was a pack of dog-eared playing cards. A bundle of letters were tied up with an old shoelace, the faded handwriting barely visible. Loose change, a pack of matches and a petrified bar of chocolate rattled around in the bottom, alongside other ephemera picked up on his travels: British beer mats, train tickets, a couple of bottle caps. There were even the obligatory photographs of ladies in varying states of undress, just as Dougie had hoped for.

'What am I looking for?' hissed Dougie, rifling through the contents and tipping the box so we could all look inside.

'Where did you get that?' whispered Ruby, the Major's pale blue hand still resting upon her chest, somehow bringing her peace and comfort.

'There was a man, Mrs Hershey,' said Dougie, glancing to me for approval. I nodded and he continued. 'Do you remember . . . Chip?'

Ruby's mask stopped misting. She froze where she lay, still as a statue. She didn't even blink.

'Flippin' Nora,' I said. 'You're the Grim Reaper! *Please* ask her to breathe!'

'Mrs Hershey?' said Dougie, and that was enough. She gulped at the air, breathing again, ragged and uneven. She closed her eyes, and through that misted mask I caught her smile.

'Captain Chip Flowers, from Columbus, Ohio.'

The Major gasped, his free hand going to his mouth to stifle the traitorous sound.

'He was my first love,' said Ruby. 'What a fellow he was. So handsome, such a rogue. He flirted with all the girls, you know? But it was just that; teasing and toying. He only had eyes for me.'

'Do you know why I'm here?' asked Dougie.

Her eyes opened again. 'I never said goodbye to him. I never told him how I truly felt.'

The Major was moving now, his hand hitting the box from below and launching the packet of playing cards into the air. The sudden, violent action took us by surprise, Dougie almost dropping the box (and his guts) with fright. The cards erupted from the tattered cardboard, exploding into the room and showering us like confetti. We looked about, watching them flutter to the floor like sycamore pods flying on the breeze. The empty playing card box landed on the bed beside Ruby. The Major reached forward and flicked its base with a forefinger. Out rolled the ring.

As teenage boys, Dougie and I had never been one for showing our emotions. First rule of the jungle: when faced with acts of great, heart-breaking love, keep it zipped. There were certain films we knew to stay away from, certainly when in the company of mates. *The Shawshank Redemption* is a fine example, a great buddy-buddy film which will have grown men weeping at the end when these two former prison inmates are reunited. Don't even go there with *Toy Story 3* – that was a cartoon and it had me reaching for the hankies. Best to claim there's something in your eye if you're ever moved to tears. Never let your pals know you're in any way empathic or have an ounce of humanity in your cold teenage heart. Never.

That said, Dougie and I now wept freely. I'm not kidding; we were a pair of babies who'd just had their teddies swiped. The ring may have appeared old and tarnished, the gold discoloured having been tucked in the bottom of a playing card box for decades, but the diamond set within it still sparkled like a star. The Major had manoeuvred around the bed and was now knelt beside it, his blue glow reflected in the gem, his face in line with Ruby's, his heartfelt words flowing fast as a waterfall.

'I'm here, my darling. I've always been here. I never left. How could I leave without saying goodbye? I swore to you that once the war was through with us, that'd be our time. When all that craziness was over, and all the dying was done, you and I would get to know one another. Turned out, all the dying wasn't done after all; I had my part to play. But I *never* stopped loving you, Ruby. In all those years, alone here with my thoughts, with other folk passing through, I never stopped thinking about you. They all went on, loved ones waiting for them in the light, but I was going nowhere without you.'

Could she hear what he was saying? I wondered. She was looking at the ring on the bed, this ring that had somehow jumped to life, out of the packet of cards, which had previously leapt from the box. I could certainly see her smiling, could see tears trickling down her wrinkled cheeks.

'Last time we spoke you called me a heel 'cause I winked at

a waitress. I was keepin' you on your toes, tryin' to get a rise out of you, and it worked. You didn't know I planned to propose to you, did you? That this ring, my mother's ring, was destined for your finger that coming weekend? It was all just me playin' games, messing with you like a darn fool. I'd never have winked if I'd known that was my last deed on this earth. Heck, I'm too charming for my own good sometimes.'

He glanced up and winked at Dougie and I. My pal was sniffing back the tears, unable to make eye contact. He wasn't alone.

'A heel, you called me! Well I'll be damned if those are the last words you ever got to say to me. We've more talkin' to do, my love, and when you're ready to chat, chinwag, bump your gums, or whatever dumb thing it is you Brits do, know this: I'll be waiting for you. I'll be here. By your side.'

Bony fingers emerged from the confines of her bedsheet and blanket, trying in vain to reach the ring. A long fingernail caught the gold band, threatening to send it off the bed and skittering into the shadows. Dougie jumped in to help, picking up the jewellery and holding it between thumb and forefinger. Ruby extended the ring finger of her left hand.

'Oh, Chip,' she whispered, her eyes fluttering again, threatening to close at any moment.

My mate looked to the Major who nodded reassuringly. Dougie held his breath and reached forward, sliding the ring over a bony knuckle until it sat snugly on Ruby's twig-like finger. If only she knew the Major was there, by her side. Could she sense him? Feel him there? Was she even truly conscious? They'd doped the poor girl up with so many drugs she probably thought it was all a dream.

'Chip.' She smiled, staring off into space. Space, it so happened, that was occupied by our American friend. It was the weirdest thing to witness: a frail old lady and a handsome young man, freeze-framed in the prime of his life.

'Dougie,' I whispered, but he needed no coaxing. He was already backing up. We turned and departed the hospital bedroom, leaving the two time-torn lovers, so close but still worlds apart.

TWENTY-FOUR

Right and Wrong

'How're you feeling, cocker?' I asked as Dougie clambered off the bus at the top of his street. He winced, wobbled and wailed a bit as he landed unsteadily on the pavement.

'I've had better days.'

'I can't think of many,' I said as the bus pulled away and into the night. 'You've foiled a bank robbery, set your old man free and reunited two star-struck lovers. All in all, that's a pretty flipping mint day's work.'

He shrugged. 'Guess you're right. I am, however, still without my girlfriend, and have the ugliest-looking scar and stitches on my shin.'

'Your leg's going to be legendary. Just imagine the tales you can tell with a war wound like that: shark attack, sword fight, mauled by a randy sixth former. Take your pick!'

Dougie chuckled as he hobbled along. He pulled his phone out, checking it for messages again. He grumbled as he pocketed it. 'I wouldn't mind getting mauled by Lucy. I miss her.'

'Give it time. She'll come round.' I wasn't sure she would, but what was the point in being maudlin on an evening like this? 'Cheer up. We can put this one in the win column.'

We turned into his drive, feeling pretty good with ourselves. The Bentley was parked out front. Maybe Mr Hancock was finally going to get it back on the road. It might have had a knackered wing – not something I'd ever forget in a hurry – but it didn't belong hidden in the garage. He'd be able to bang that panel out again, fix the crack in the windscreen no problem. I reckoned he owed his boy a long drive in the sunshine. He'd been a changed man when we left that morning. I had such hope for the pair of them. It was a new dawn in their relationship. I hoped to goodness this was the start of something glorious between father and son.

'It's a nice feeling, doing the right thing, isn't it?' said Dougie as he stepped up to the front door, putting his key in the lock.

'Doesn't happen often. We should savour it.'

'Odd,' he said, giving the door a gentle nudge. It swung open. 'Silly old sod's left it open.' Dougie stepped into the house, while I paused on the threshold. For a fleeting moment, I felt a chill descend. I glanced at the car, that crumpled wing beside me. I turned back to the door, still unsettled as I followed him.

'You there, Dad?' shouted Dougie.

'Dougie,' I said, my sense of unease growing now at a frightening rate. He waved his hand to me, trying to shush me as he continued to call to his dad.

'Sorry I'm late. Had to go to the hospital. Cut my leg playing football.' He turned into the lounge, pushing the glass-panelled door open. 'You won't believe the number of stitch—'

His words were cut short by the sight that awaited him.

The lounge had been a pigsty for months now, but it was a mess we'd grown accustomed to. Chaos had since visited the room in terrible fashion. The television set lay on its side, the picture flickering. The mirror above the fireplace was smashed, the heirloom carriage clock busted on the floor, lying on a bed of shining glass shards. Mr Hancock lay slumped in his armchair. No change there, one might have thought, but he was in an awful state. His face was battered and bloodied, his right eye puffy and swollen shut. His lips were split, and when he saw his son enter the room he immediately started moving, raising his hands in warning, burbling through bloodied teeth.

'Look out!' I shouted, but too late.

The figure who had been hiding in the shadows behind the door had emerged fast, sucker-punching Dougie from behind, right in the kidneys. He went down like a sack of spuds, hitting the cluttered carpet with a crunch, his face millimetres away from the daggers of broken mirror. Mr Hancock rose from the chair on unsteady legs, desperate to help his son.

'Sit down,' said Bradbury, booting Mr Hancock in the chest. The poor man flew back, sprawling back into the tatty old chair with a wheezing wail. 'You don't know when you're done, do you, George?'

Bradbury turned his attention to Dougie. 'You came home at the wrong time, didn't you, sport? Your dad and I were having a wee chat. He's been a bad lad, y'see? Been talking to the rozzers, hasn't he? I can't have that. I can't be having my people being . . . *disloyal*.'

What was I doing? I was frozen, a statue, a spectral spectator in my killer's company. The last time I'd encountered him I'd been unaware of his horrific crime. There had been something between us though, for sure. I knew Bradbury had been a bad man as sure as night followed day. He was a wrong'un, as my own dad would say. And he'd reacted to my presence as well; an imperceptible turn my way, as if catching me fleetingly in the corner of his eye. Once more he glanced across his shoulder in my direction; could he sense me there, so close?

'Leave him alone.' Dougie's words were a mumble, a murmur as he inched along on his belly. With his hands beneath him, he reminded me of a helpless worm, squirming away from Bradbury, across the broken glass. 'Murderer.'

I heard what he said, but for a moment I thought the Liverpudlian had missed it. His reply told me otherwise.

'What've you been saying, George? You been spreading nasty rumours?' Mr Hancock sobbed as Bradbury loomed over him. 'You just can't keep your mouth shut, can you? Your lad, the coppers; anybody else you've been flapping those fat lips to? You let some good men down last night. Good thing I let Monty take my place on the job or it could've been *me* banged up with those poor saps.'

I closed my eyes as Bradbury struck Mr Hancock, a volley of blows clattering the man in the chair. Punches rained down, each one smacking home with a sickening crunch. I was frozen, the most hideous feeling descending. On previous occasions, when faced with such emotional situations, I'd been spurred into action, able to add my strength to Dougie's fight. That talent had escaped me. I was Samson after a trip to the barber. Whatever powers I had were gone, and I could feel the life being choked from me all over again. I was a ghost; I didn't *need* to breathe. Yet somehow, the longer I remained in Bradbury's presence, the more I seemed to fade. Impossibly, I was gasping for air. I looked at my hands, vanishing before my eyes, the essence dissipating, the blue glow dying.

'Leave him!' shouted Dougie, his voice cracking where he lay prone. 'He never told the police! I did!'

The attack abruptly ceased, Bradbury's bloodied fists

wavering motionless above Mr Hancock. The man turned slowly, looking down at my pal. While I was fading, Bradbury was growing stronger.

'You what?' he whispered, but Dougie didn't answer. He was looking at me from where he lay on his tummy, face peppered with studs of mirror.

'Will,' he gasped.

My connection with the living world was weakening, as was my hold over my phantom form. My hands were losing their integrity, wisps of smoke peeling away as I struggled to keep myself together. I cast my mind back to our old friend Phyllis, the phantom girl who had befriended me when I'd first become a ghost. In her killer's presence she'd gone through the same thing, unable to fight back. History was repeating, only this time it was me having my un-life choked from me.

'*You* told the cops?' hissed Bradbury. He gave Dougie a prod with the toe of his boot. 'I've got you to thank for this? My world turning to crap?' He nudged him again, harder now. 'What's up, sport? Cat got your tongue? Not so cocky now, eh?' He kicked Dougie, my mate doubling up into a foetal position.

'Fight back, Dougie,' I said, my voice almost lost on that same strange wind that was causing my fragile body to break apart. I tried to focus my mind, concentrate on keeping my shape, but it was hopeless. I was going. This was the end.

‘Here’s what’s gonna happen, George,’ said Bradbury as he kicked my friend. ‘You’re gonna watch me beat your boy to a pulp. Then I’m going to beat you to a pulp. After that, I’ll have your keys, lock the door and take that nice car.’

He wasn’t even looking at Dougie, too busy goading Mr Hancock. I could hardly hear the words, my body barely present, my mind holding on to Dougie’s world by the most slender of threads.

‘Maybe they’ll find the two of you in a few weeks. Your next-door neighbour will notice the whiff, eh? You ever smelled a dead body, George? They make an awful stink in summer. Especially two of ’em.’

Dougie rolled over on to his back after the last kick. In one hand he held his mobile phone, but it was his other hand that drew my attention, hauling me back from the brink. It flew through the air, up and towards Bradbury. The dagger of splintered mirror sank deep into the killer’s right thigh as Dougie dragged it down, separating fancy black suit and the flesh beneath. His own fingers were bleeding but he paid them no heed, releasing his hold on the blade when it would travel no further. He scrambled clear, screaming into the phone.

‘Are you getting this?’ he shouted between ragged sobs. He was a mess, a beaten-up replica of his poor father. ‘Please, come quick! It’s Bradbury. We’re at 18 Woollacombe Close.’

Bradbury screamed as he collapsed on one leg, hauling himself upright as his hands scrambled across the mantelpiece. Bloodied fingers found Mr Hancock's keyring, snatching them up and curling them into a fist. The other hand reached down and tugged the jagged blade out of his thigh. It came away with a wet squelch and a gurgled cry from the killer. He laughed hysterically before lifting his head up, glancing into the fractured remains of the mirror. The laughter stopped instantly, his face going terribly slack as he caught sight of his reflection.

As Dougie had sprung into action, the change had occurred. Perhaps his valiant stand gave me the strength, I'd been inspired by him; we'd never know. At that final moment, about to blink out of existence, I'd arrived at a crossroads: burn out or fade away. I'd gone with the former. Fear of Bradbury had changed to outrage, nerves giving way to confidence. It wasn't revenge I sought for the man's wickedness. If this was to be my final act, I wanted justice. I wanted him to *know* that there were consequences to his actions. I wanted him to *know* what he'd done to me. I shone like a bright blue sentinel. I kid you not, I was a superhero. I was Doc Manhattan from *Watchmen.*

Bradbury saw me behind him in the broken mirror. If I'd expected a grand stand-off between myself and the man that killed me, it never came. That stuff's just in the movies. This is the point when the hero says something really cool and clever, a few well-chosen words that make you punch the air with glee. I had no such banter in the locker. I simply stood there and looked at him. And my God, did he ever see me. As sure as Dougie could, Bradbury saw me in all my ghostly glory. I think he might have peed his pants at that moment, judging by the dark strain that spread through those ruined fancy trousers. He hurdled Mr Hancock and the armchair, taking a circuitous route around the lounge, climbing the walls to keep distance from me.

And that was when she finally arrived. She certainly picked her moments.

'Dougie?' asked Lucy as she walked through the hall from the open front door. 'Are you there? You're right. We need to talk . . .' She craned her head into the lounge.

'Get out of here!' shouted Dougie from where he lay in a beaten heap, but Bradbury was already moving. He bounced off the lounge door, shattering the marbled glass as he ricocheted into the hall. Lucy was running, crying out as the killer went after her. But I was already crouching over Dougie, wondering what I could do to help him.

'Get up, numbnuts,' I said. 'You need to go after him. You have to stop him!'

Dougie shook his head, a bloodied hand clutching his stomach, the other still holding the mobile in a kung fu grip. We could hear the police on the other end, asking questions, trying to keep him on the line. His head lolled, bouncing back off the sofa as he fought to stay conscious.

'Dougie! Stay with me! Lucy needs you! I can't do this without you!'

I heard more screaming outside, followed by the Bentley's engine gunning into life. Mr Hancock slid from his chair, crawling across the floor to his boy. He couldn't hear me, couldn't see me, but he knew his son was in pain. I stood to one side as he cradled his boy in his arms.

'You can,' whispered Dougie, managing one more word before he passed out. 'Muppet.'

I stepped away from the Hancocks and turned directly toward the front windows of the lounge. I saw the Bentley pull away down the road, speeding off into the summer night. I walked away from Dougie, through the wall and the window pane, out into the street. I slowed, taking tentative steps. I walked on, wincing, waiting for our bond to catch me about the belly, pull me back like a bungee. It never happened. Where had the umbilical tether gone?

I was running now, down the street, through the darkness. I was the T-1000. Unstoppable. Dead I might have been, but I'd never felt more alive. Then I was flying, straight as an arrow, closing in on my quarry.

My world had turned on its head. I was connected to Dougie no longer.

I was tied to Bradbury and the Bentley that killed me.

TWENTY-FIVE

Crime and Punishment

The Bentley might not have been driven for eight months, but it still ran like a dream and purred like a lion cub. I followed in its wake as it tore up the road, reeling myself in like a demented water-skier. For every metre of tarmac the car covered, I stole two, closing the distance relentlessly. I flew along after it, drawn inexorably like a moth to the flame. My whole being was aglow with strength and purpose – head and heart, guts and glory. Houses and trees blurred in my periphery, cars and pedestrians fading away until only the Bentley was in my sights.

Freshly awakened from its grim hibernation, the car was king of the road once more, a majestic beast roaring through the night. Streetlights bounced off the polished black paintwork, flickering like fireflies as they danced over bonnet, roof and boot. The rear bumper vibrated as I approached, its curved chrome a shining scimitar, the car as connected to me as the killer who drove it. I spied the figure in the back seat, her head slumped against the left passenger window. My hands extended, bright blue and burning with urgency, reaching out as the road rushed by beneath me. Before I could connect, the Bentley took a hard right, switching direction down St Mary's Road. I charged on, out and away from it, hurtling headlong into a row of terraced houses at the top of the street.

I didn't slow down. Instead, I rode the corner, taking a curve of my own like a speedway racer whilst remaining aware of the disappearing Bentley. I hit the first house and phased through its wall, riding through and into the next house, again and again, room after room, scene after scene flitting through my vision. One home after another zipped by; a family watching the television, a babysitter on the phone with her boyfriend, a bachelor eating his meal alone, an amorous couple on a sofa, a dog licking its bum. The mutt barked at my brief cameo; something else to add to the *Rules of Ghosting* perhaps? That one could wait. I emerged out of the end terrace, back into the night, riding the bend and briefly traversing the street.

I rocketed through the graveyard, parallel to the road, never more in tune with my powers. I felt jacked up on spook juice, a supercharged supernatural. Stirred by my passing, the occasional never-before-encountered phantom shimmered into view, rising from the grave like a spectral somnambulist. As much as I would've loved to stop and chat, pick their brains about the afterlife, now really wasn't the time. My current strength was drawn from Bradbury and the Bentley. I had only one appointment this night, and that was with the stone-cold, very alive killer who held my best mate's girlfriend hostage.

I emerged from the graveyard, catching up with the Bentley once more as it approached the crossroads at the bottom of St Mary's Road. Somewhere nearby I could hear the wail of police sirens, but there was no sign of the accompanying blue lights. The traffic signals were changing, green shifting through amber to red. The Bentley gunned it, tyres screeching as it accelerated into the junction. The car leapt across the intersection, cutting up the traffic that was already proceeding across its path. Horns blared, cars swerved and collided as Bradbury hurtled through the stream of vehicles, regardless of the chaos he caused. He would kill someone else at this rate, of that I had no doubt. I closed the gap; three metres, two metres, my hands reaching once more as I sought to connect with the fleeing Bentley. I felt a bolt course through me, an electric shock as my fingers brushed the chrome, and then I was inside the vehicle, shifting through the boot before emerging in the rear passenger seat.

Lucy's head bounced off the window, her neck crooked

where she'd been flung into the car. She was concussed, unconscious, her body tangled in a seatbelt Mr Hancock had fitted. Her body jiggled as the Bentley bounced along, its driver oblivious to the condition of his passenger. I brought my attention to Bradbury, his wiry body hunched over the wheel. He looked up into the rear-view mirror and, not for the first time that night, didn't like what he saw. Neither did I.

The world could have stopped at that moment for all I knew. I saw him utterly for what he was, his eyes as black as the Bentley's bodywork. They were the dull, dead eyes of a shark, a killer's gaze. The shark got a bad press; it killed to eat. Bradbury shared no such honest compulsion. They say the eyes are the window into the soul; Bradbury didn't have one.

'You,' he said, dark eyes blinking. 'But . . . I *killed* you!'

'So you did, sport,' I replied. 'Seems you did a poor job. How's that leg holding up?'

'You . . . you can't be there. I'm having a . . . a . . . hallucination or a vision.'

'If this is a vision then it's a bitch, isn't it?'

'I'm dreaming,' he said, choking on the words. 'This is a nightmare.'

'A nightmare, for sure, but one of your making, you murdering swine.'

Bradbury had heard enough. He swerved the wheel suddenly, as if he could send me flying from the car. The Bentley lurched from side to side, yet I remained seated, connected to the car as if it were Dougie. Lucy bounced about once more, her head banging off the window again. I was worried for her; who knew what he'd done to leave her senseless in the back seat.

'Give up, Bradbury,' I said, cutting the banter. My voice came out as a hiss, cold breath chilling his neck. I saw the goosebumps race across his skin, my murderer twitching and flinching with every icy word. Over his shoulder, I could see the keys swinging in the ignition.

'You're not getting away. The police are after you. How far do you think you'll get?'

He blinked, wiping his eyes with the back of a bloodied hand. He was muttering to himself now, his speech fast and fevered. If I reached forward, could I grab the keys? Rip them out? It wasn't the same as the push I could do on Dougie, those rare moments when we could physically connect, but then again this was no ordinary situation. I felt every ounce of righteous rage coursing through my body. I was convinced I could do anything. Slowly I phased through the driver's seat, beginning to slide through his twitching body. The sensation was nauseating for me; the devil knew how hideous it was for Bradbury.

'Turn yourself in,' I said, my voice echoing in his head. 'Let the girl go. Stop running.'

'This can't be happening,' he was saying, hitting himself in the temple with his fist. 'This can't be happening. I'm dreaming. Wake up, fella. It's just a dream. If I jolt myself enough, I'll wake up.'

I was reaching forward, through him, towards the keys, but I could sense he was grinning. The side of his face curling up as I slid through, contorting into a hideous Joker smile. He whispered the last words before I could grab the keys.

'Wake up.'

He turned the wheel hard and held it fast as we were approaching the incline towards the railway bridge. The big old oak on the right-hand side of the road was suddenly illuminated by the Bentley's headlights. I changed my tack, seizing the steering wheel instead, my hands fitting over his, blue fingers closing over his white-knuckled grasp. I yanked hard, back the other way, every ounce of will and determination pouring into the deed. The wheel spun left, our hands fused together as the Bentley lurched back the other way as it rode across the bridge. Now it was the stone wall that was lit by the lamp's beams, as we crashed into red brick and out into the space beyond.

Ordinarily, one's life flashes before one's eyes in a near-death moment like this, freezing people into inaction. I was hindered by no such sense of mortality. I turned and leapt into the back seat, phasing through a screaming Bradbury and his seat as the Bentley began nose-diving through the air over the wall. We were accompanied by a shower of broken masonry as we plummeted toward the railway line below. Lucy was a ragdoll, a loose collection of flesh and bone that would be pulverised at the moment of impact. I threw myself over her as the Bentley rolled, hitting the embankment once, twice, before bouncing and grinding to a screeching halt on the tracks.

I slowly brought my face up and looked around the wrecked car. The Bentley had been transformed into a mass of twisted metal and splintered wood, interiors buckled and broken. Steam hissed from the radiator, sparks spluttering from the exposed engine beyond the shattered windscreen. Bradbury was folded over the wheel, lifeless, his thick mop of curly black hair matted with blood. I looked down at Lucy, the door that she'd rested upon now missing, torn off in the crash. I had enveloped her body with my own, protecting her as if my life depended upon it. I had felt her heartbeat, heard her breathing, could have sworn blind that I could smell her hair. That was how strong the emotions were that had surged through my body at that moment.

I heard the train before I saw it. The wreck was straddling the tracks, and those thick lengths of steel now hummed into life, singing with the train's approach. The light appeared, through the bridge's dark arch in the distance, dim but growing fast. With no more thought I seized hold of Lucy and channelled my energies, 'pulling' instead of 'pushing', dragging her from the vehicle. The Bentley had been the death of me; I wouldn't let it take her life as well. Ghostly power coursed through me as I dragged her clear of the wreckage and up on to the embankment.

Then I heard him sobbing.

Bradbury was alive! I drifted back to the busted car, peering through the cracked windows and ripped upholstery. His head lolled as he looked up, dazed and confused. The approaching train lights bounced through the night toward us. His cry was pitiful, and I couldn't help but reply.

'Get out of there,' I hissed, urging him to free himself.

He looked my way through the tangle of metal. 'My belt,' he whimpered. 'It's stuck. Please, you have to help me!'

As quandaries go, it was the biggie, but my dear mum had raised me right. Torn I might have been, but not half as torn as if I'd left him to die there. I shifted through the wreck and spied the problem. The gearbox had been ripped out of the engine block, spearing him to his seat through a frayed strap of belt.

'It won't come loose,' he cried, shaking the worn leather frantically, his grip slippery with blood.

'Let me,' I said, throwing my hands over his, applying the same pressure as I had with the steering wheel. We both concentrated, he with his human strength and me with my spectral. I closed my eyes, willing the leather to tear, feeling the power ripple from my chest, down through my arms and into my fingers. The train whistle sounded as it approached the station, an express. Not stopping. The leather snapped and I drifted clear with the effort, exhausted with the spent energy.

'Go!' I yelled. 'Quickly!'

As good ghostly intentions went, mine were up there with the best, surely guaranteeing me a pass through the pearly gates should the opportunity ever arise again. Sadly, not all ghosts are cut from the same cloth. Bradbury didn't see him as he kicked open the driver's door, the train almost upon him. Nor did he catch sight of the flame at the end of that long, dark pole, emerging from the dark arch of the railway bridge like the lure of an angler fish. But when the skeletal body and stovepipe hat separated from the shadows and danced toward the wreck, Bradbury saw the Lamplighter alright. The phantom was silhouetted by the onrushing light, terrible eyes burning with wicked glee. Bradbury tried to rise from the wreckage, screamed for help, for forgiveness, but it was too late.

The Lamplighter leapt, the train whistle screaming at his back, his limbs twisting into impossible positions. Pinning Bradbury back into the Bentley, the spectre burbled over his victim like a hideous, hungry spider. My killer's cries were of pure, unadulterated terror; not at his impending death, but the promise in the Lamplighter's blazing gaze of horror and hell that awaited him in the great and grim beyond. I turned away as train hit car, Bradbury's bloodcurdling screams carried away down the tracks along with the Bentley.

TWENTY-SIX

Loving and Leaving

The children's ward was a peculiar place after dark. By day, there was a positivity that was missing elsewhere in the hospital. Perhaps it was the unrelenting chipperness of youth, the glass half-full mentality that the older, more poorly patients struggled to capture. The relentless blare of computer games and duelling televisions rang out down the halls. Sure, there were some ill kids there – and I'm talking *really* ill – but even they managed to find the fun between the traumas and treatments. However, come nightfall it was lights out. Electronic mischief was banned and a curfew called on capering. The quiet was broken by crying, sobs splitting the silence and echoing down dark corridors. Away from home, from parents, sick and scared; as sleepover venues go, hospitals rarely make the list.

I stood at the foot of Dougie's bed, watching him sleep. Not so unusual; I'd spent the last eight months doing that very thing, permanently awake while he slumbered. That's a ghost's lot in un-life. We don't get to sleep. A living human being would be driven insane having to endure my nightly routine. But for me, it was part of the gig. Dougie's present condition wasn't, though. Patched up, head bandaged, wired up with a drip in his arm; there was no getting used to seeing my best mate like that. It hurt like hell just to look at him, but I couldn't pull my eyes away. I wouldn't leave him alone. I wanted to be there when he woke up. He was going to wake up, wasn't he?

'There's a special word for a guy like you.'

I turned to find the Major stood behind me, just off my shoulder. I shrugged sheepishly. 'I'm no hero.'

'I was going to go with Jonah. It's like you're *cursed* or something! How many loved ones can you get into one hospital?'

I appreciated the gentle ribbing. I missed it with my regular tormentor, Dougie, out of action.

'How's he doing?' asked the American.

'He's sleeping a lot, which is understandable. Overheard what the doctors said; he has broken ribs and a fractured skull. Bradbury really put the boot in. Plus he's popped the stitches on his shin, silly sod.'

'Jeez, he really went to bat for his pa, didn't he?'

I nodded. 'Saved Mr Hancock from an even worse beating. He's paying for it now, though.'

'He's alive, ain't he? That's something. And his old man?'

'He's in a ward in the east wing.'

'A family affair, huh?'

'He's been kicking off with them, wanting to come over and see his son. Sounds like they'll wheel him over in the morning.'

'You went over to see him?'

'Yeah. Like Dougie, he's in a bad way. Right leg in a brace and suspended over his bed. Busted kneecap, broken fingers and a dislocated jaw. I swear, they're both lucky to be alive.'

'And the femme fatale . . .?'

'Femme-what now?' I said, before realising who he was on about. I blushed. 'Oh. You're on about Lucy.'

She was in another of the children's wards, her folks having ensured she had a private room. I wasn't entirely sure what it all meant for her relationship with Dougie. I'd a good idea though, having caught the glowering looks and furious words Mr Carpenter had unleashed upon arriving at the hospital and hearing reports of the night's events. His daughter's abduction followed by near-death crash and subsequent train-car-inferno were not going to reflect well on my pal. It was safe to assume Dougie and Lucy's romantic adventure was firmly up in the air.

'I heard the nurses say she'd be out tomorrow. Seems she's doing better than anyone. Probably a blessing she's suffering amnesia.'

'So you went over there, to old man Hancock and your buddy's beau without Sparky here?' The Major looked impressed.

'Yeah, a weird thing happened. Seems I'm not tied to Dougie any more. Whatever kept us together like Siamese twins seems to have upped and vamoosed. It was when Bradbury turned up at the Hancock house. Something switched in my head. The minute Dougie fought back I realised why I was still here, *who* I was supposed to be haunting. Following my mate night and day had led me to his father and the Bentley, and ultimately to Bradbury. He was the one I was meant to haunt all along.'

'And he's gone now,' said the Major, patting my back. 'How do you feel about that?'

How *did* I feel? I hadn't given it much thought, being too preoccupied with my friend's fate. Those odd occasions when I'd thought back to that awful night left me nauseous. The beatings, the car crash, the Lamplighter and Bradbury's screams. I may have been a ghost but those scenes would haunt me to the end of my days, whenever they finally came.

'I try not to think about it.'

'Understandable. But what of your tricksy predicament?

With all that's passed and the bad man dead and gone? How do you feel now?'

'Kind of ... empty, I suppose. If I expected his death to bring some kind of closure, I was mistaken. If anything, it's just thrown up more questions.'

'Like what?'

'Well, why haven't I moved on? I thought my killer's demise might be my ticket out of here. But here I am, going nowhere fast. I was convinced that if I solved my death and set wrongs to rights that I'd be sorted. Bang! Out of here. Yet here I sit, still waiting for the call.'

The Major sighed. 'Son, I don't have the answers, I'm afraid.'

I chuckled. 'You never do. Unless the question pertains to swing music, retro hair products or the films of Jimmy Cagney—'

'Up to and including summer of 1943,' he added. 'I'm not so strong with my movie trivia after that ...'

'Funny that,' I said, twigging the reference to his own untimely death. 'I wonder what happened to him.'

'Who?'

'Bradbury.'

'He's dead, ain't he? Couldn't have happened to a nicer guy.'

I shook my head. 'But where did he *end up*? What's *his* punishment for all the terrible things he did in his life? Does he simply blink out of existence, swallowed by death's vast darkness?'

'Cheery thought.'

'Or is there a reckoning? Does he pay for those crimes?'

The Major clicked his teeth ruefully. 'I like to think that a monster like the Lamplighter knows exactly what he's doing. There'll be a special place in hell for Bradbury, kid, don't you worry about that.'

I shuddered at the thought. 'Is that it then?'

'What do you mean, Will?'

'This. Us. Being here, left behind. Did we not tick all the boxes for the big guy upstairs? Did we come up short when the winners' names were read out? Why else would we be cursed to stay here in limbo when others can move on?'

'We're not *cursed*, Will,' said the Major, seizing me by the arms and turning me so we were face to face. 'This is a gift, son. A second bite at the apple, if you will. We're not being punished. We have a job to do. We're left here to do some *good*.'

'And the Lamplighter?'

'Well,' the Major shrugged. 'Different big guys leave different agents behind to do their work. But never doubt that you serve a purpose here.'

'Which is what?'

'Damned if I know,' said the Yank. 'Which brings me to

this.' He hugged me, hard. Well, as hard as one ethereal being can hug another.

'What was that for?' I grunted.

'That's goodbye,' he said, pulling away and straightening my trailing scarf. 'You're gonna be OK, you hear?'

'I don't follow,' I said, ever slow on the uptake. A second later and I understood all.

She stood at the end of the corridor by the lift, waiting for him. Like us, she shone with the same, pale blue hue. Oddly, though, she wasn't a frail old lady any more. I didn't know how any of this ghosting nonsense worked. I probably never would. Ruby Hershey was young again, her stylish hair tied up, her hospital nightgown replaced by a vintage polkadot dress. She smiled at me and waved. The Major waved back.

'Ain't she a picture?' he whispered, his grin dazzling.

'She's that and then some.' I wasn't lying. If the Major thought he could've been a movie star, then the flickering image of Ruby Hershey could've just stepped out of the silver screen. If I wandered the planet to the end of time I'd never see a more beautiful woman.

'How do I look?' he asked, jutting his jaw out and dusting down his uniform. It was my turn to straighten his tie.

'Like a million dollars. Now go kiss your girl.'

He walked into the corridor, turning on his heel as if he were on parade. Ahead, behind Ruby, the lift doors slid open, revealing an incredible light within. It bathed the woman entirely, almost swallowing her right there and then, but she was going nowhere. She was waiting for her man. Ruby extended a hand and beckoned him. The Major paused, and looked back to me. He clicked his fingers.

'What?' I said.

'Y'know . . . you could join us.'

'Join you?'

'Of course,' he said, a look of sheer bloody-minded joy illuminating his face. 'What's stopping you?'

Good lord. He was right. What *was* stopping me? Here was my chance, the thing that I'd missed the night I'd died. I was already walking, leaving the ward and heading into the corridor.

'Do you think they'll mind?' I asked, unsure of who "they" even were.

'What's the worst they can do? Chuck you out on the ground floor? Come on, Will. Step in line and leave the talking to me.'

He winked.

I laughed.

He set off toward Ruby and the light, me just off his shoulder. The closer we got to the glowing doorway, the more I was enveloped by its radiating warmth. It was the sun and I was a speck of sand on the beach. I could swear, at that moment, beyond that magical portal, I could hear the sea lapping upon a distant shore. I could hear *Yellow Bird* being played by a steel band, accompanied by merrymaking and laughter. Turns out heaven was Antigua. The Major walked ahead of me, looking back when he noticed I'd stopped.

'What?' he asked, the smile slipping.

'I can't.'

'You . . . can't? Of course you can. Here, take my hand.'

He extended it toward me. I could just seize it, right there and then, let myself get led out of there. But that wasn't who I was. It isn't who I am.

'Unfinished business,' I whispered. Now it was his turn to catch *my* drift.

'Ah,' he said, looking past me, back down the corridor to the ward we'd departed. The ward in which my best friend lay in a fitful, troubled sleep. 'Unfinished business.'

'It's not just Dougie.'

'Then what? You do *want* to move on, don't you? On to something better? Brighter?'

'You know what,' I said with a smile. 'I'm not sure I do.'

The Major looked dumbstruck.

'Everybody's been banging on about how I should move on to the next world, wave goodbye to limbo, when the truth of the matter is nobody ever asked me what *I* wanted. I'm a teenager, Chip, or at least *was* before I died. My time on earth had been fleeting, blink-and-you'll-miss-it. It was only just beginning and then –' I snapped my fingers '– it was finished. Snuffed out. That'd be game over for most anybody else, but for whatever reason – Dougie, his father, Bradbury – I got another bite at the apple.

'I may be dead but I'm not done living. There's still stuff I can do here. I can *help* people, be they alive *or* mortally challenged. You showed me more than anyone that one can have a purpose in un-life. And besides, it looks like there might be a vacancy here . . .'

I winked at the Major and he smiled back. Removing his US Air Force peaked cap he passed it across, dropping it on to my head. It was the strangest sensation, the ghostly object feeling as real to me as a corporeal item against one's flesh. I hooked my thumb and pushed the visor up and out of my eyes so he could see my grin. The baton had been passed. The Major snapped his heels and made a sharp salute.

'It's been my absolute pleasure to serve with you, Will Underwood.'

'Shake a tail-feather, Yank. You're keeping your date waiting.'

He turned and walked into the light, the doorway already narrowing, drawing them both in. I had to turn away, the sheer intensity blinding me. If I'd had eyeballs they'd be pooling in their sockets. And like that, it was gone. The corridor was dark again, the gloom only broken by the occasional flickering ceiling light or a nursing station computer monitor. I backed up, returning to the foot of my best mate's bed. If there'd been a chair, I'd have sat in it. Instead I climbed on to the bed and lay down beside my dear friend.

'Muppet.'

I closed my eyes and listened to Dougie breathe. I tried to remember what it felt like. To sleep. To dream.

TWENTY-SEVEN

Meet and Greet

'You look like a right plum in that.'

'You're just jealous,' I replied, running my thumb along the visor's edge of the Major's dress hat. 'I reckon I look a dude. You can try it on but somehow I don't think it'll fit you.'

'Still can't believe he left without saying goodbye.'

Dougie and I stared across the rose garden as the sick and their visitors shambled about in the drizzle, searching for somewhere to shelter. These were the hardcore smokers, unable to go longer than an hour without sneaking out for a sly puff. Overcoats were donned and umbrellas were hoisted as they got their sweet cancerous kicks in the rain. They'd be back here soon enough, some of them. Judging by the terrible coughing of the odd one, they probably wouldn't be leaving.

'Like I said, the Major wasn't really in a position where he could hang about for you to get your arse out of bed. It was a bit of a one-time-ticket. Trust me, they don't hold the door open for you if you dally.'

We were stood beneath the ambulance canopy outside A&E, waiting for Mr Hancock to turn up. It had been two weeks since the accident, and in that time there had been plenty of rest and recuperation for Dougie to sink his teeth into. To be fair, he'd gorged on it, spending a ridiculous amount of time with his feet up as the nurses reached, fetched and carried for him. Stu Singer, Andy Vaughn and even Bloody Mary had proved to be invaluable mates, visiting frequently and bringing a plethora of goodies in from home to amuse him: comics, books, iPad and even Dougie's mobile phone. That stash had been tricky to retrieve, with both Dougie and his dad in hospital, but everybody's favourite head-the-ball was a resourceful lad; while Andy kept watch, Stu had gone in through the garage, jimmying the locked door to the kitchen before sweeping up all that was needed. God bless the sons of vicars.

'Besides,' I said, 'he might have been fond of you in a chalk and cheese kinda way, but you were no Ruby. More of a nugget of coal in comparison.'

'Really? She must've polished up nicely then. Last I saw of the old dear she looked her age.'

'That's the weird thing. Look at me in my torn jeans, winter coat and Doctor Who scarf; I'm still wearing the clothes I carked it in. No doubt I will until I finally – if ever – get my chance to leave. It wasn't the same Ruby waiting for the Major though. She was a young woman, in all her splendour.'

'Splendour?'

'Sounds showy, doesn't it? Not on this occasion. She was a knockout. They made a mighty fine couple.'

'Perhaps your apparition is linked to your mood? It was the happiest moment of your life when you died, wasn't it? Lousy timing, I know.'

'Perhaps those years when she was first with the Major, so long ago, were when Ruby was at her happiest. That'd make sense, wouldn't it? Either way, it'd be nice to change the outfit now and again. I suppose the Major's cap is something.'

'Something else to go in the *Rules of Ghosting* notebook.'

'You're keeping it up to date, aren't you?'

'Course I am,' he lied, glancing at his phone.

'Anything?'

'No,' he said, glumly.

Barely a moment had gone by in the last week where I hadn't found him checking his mobile for messages. He'd sent a bunch of them to Lucy, asking to speak with her. There was a ton of stuff the two of them needed to talk through. Most of it Dougie had been reluctant to discuss on account of Bradbury – his dad, the car, the villain himself – but with that monster out of the picture it freed up everything. Nothing was off topic, but it was just his luck that Mr Carpenter had apparently put a kibosh on their relationship. Whether she was receiving my pal's plaintive messages, we couldn't know. Perhaps her dad had confiscated the phone and was fuming each and every frequent moment it pinged: *message received!* I hadn't the heart to tell Dougie about the mood Mr Carpenter had been in after the accident. I was looking for the right moment, but it hadn't yet arrived.

'I'm sure she'll get back to you, mate,' I said, patting him on the back. He felt the contact. 'Just give her a bit of time, eh? Play it cool, Sparky.'

We both laughed, thinking of our departed American friend.

'Do you think he's happy, wherever they went?' asked Dougie.

'He's with Ruby. Wherever they went, even if it was just that blinding light and then nothing, it'll be heavenly for him.'

'So that was heaven, then? The light in the lift?'

'It was heaven for our friend,' I said. 'Might be something different when yours or my time comes.'

'You could've gone with him, y'know?' He was avoiding eye contact with me, searching the road for the approach of his dad. 'You didn't have to hang about for me.'

'You would've moaned like a whiny baby if I'd scarpered,

and you know it. Nah, I wasn't about to skedaddle and leave you in the lurch. It's not what friends do. Not after what we've been through.'

He didn't say anything, and he didn't need to. Our friendship was pretty damn special, that bond keeping us together in spite of a piddling thing like death. Dougie being the kind of lad he was, chose that moment to let loose a wee parp. It did the trick, repelling me like magic.

'You cheapen everything,' I said.

He chuckled, but I caught the briefest look. He nodded, ever so slightly. It was the closest I'd get to genuine emotion, and I was happy to take it. The approach of a car Mr Hancock had commandeered broke the mood, and not a second too soon. We were dangerously close to telling one another how we really felt, and that would *never* do for teenage boys. It would've caused a distortion in the space time continuum. Or something.

Mr Hancock opened the passenger door of the beaten-up old estate car and beckoned his son.

'Who does *that* hunk of junk belong to?' asked Dougie warily from where he sheltered from the grim shower.

'Reverend Singer,' said his dad. 'He called and asked if there was any way he could help. What a nice chap. Been so long since I'd accepted the help of others, I'd forgotten it could even happen. And let's face it, I think the Bentley's breathed its last.'

Dougie and I smiled as his dad turned his attention to the car radio, searching for a vintage station. My mate had asked Stu to let his father know Mr Hancock might need a helping hand getting back on his feet again, return the chaos of his life to something that resembled order. The good reverend had wasted no time and Mr Hancock had happily taken the bait. The man who has friends is a wealthy fellow indeed.

Dougie set off through the puddles towards the car, messenger bag across the shoulder full of comics, books and techno goodies. He lobbed it through the door and into the back seat before turning back to me. I remained standing beneath the canopy, watching my friend through the relentless summer shower.

'What are you doing?' mouthed Dougie. 'Our ride's here. I want to go home. I've spent more than enough time in this blooming building.'

'You go.'

'Eh?' Dougie looked at me as if I'd just grown another head. 'What are you on about? Go?'

'I'm staying.'

Dougie stomped across the rain-slicked pavement and tipped his head to one side, so much so I feared it might fall off.

'Since when did you have an option?'

'Since Bradbury. Dougie, I'm not *bound* to anyone any

more. Once I chased after him that night, I had a new target for my attention. And when he died . . . well, I appear to have been left to my own devices, like a fart on the breeze.'

'A ghost without a host.'

'Something like that.'

Dougie was quiet, thinking it through. He looked disappointed.

'I thought you'd be happy. You've been bumping your gums for months now about how you don't get a moment's privacy. You can't take a dump in peace, so you tell me. Isn't this what you wanted?'

'I thought so. But now it's happened, I'm not so sure. Maybe I got used to you, Will.'

'That's sweet.'

'Let me finish – got used to you like athlete's foot.'

'Again with the cheapening.' It was enough to lighten the mood. I could sense he was upset, but I'd had plenty of time to think about this.

'So if you're not coming with me, what's your plan?'

'For starters, this doesn't mean I'm done with you. Gonna have to check out how this solo spectral shenanigan works, see if I can flutter my way to Casa Hancock as soon as I get a chance. You're my best mate. You won't get rid of me that easily.'

He brightened at that, the old grin reappearing.

'But where will you go?'

I looked around at the entrance to the A&E, peered down the road as another ambulance approached, its blue lights flashing. Its siren whooped as it drew closer, urging Mr Hancock to shift the estate car.

'I hear there's an opening here in the meet and greet department. Be nice to give something back after all the Major did for us.'

'All the Major did for us?' exclaimed Dougie. 'He was all goofy teeth and quiff, all mouth and no trousers! He couldn't pass a mirror without winking at himself!'

I grinned. 'You know he loved you, don't you?'

Dougie threw me a two-fingered salute and set off towards his dad's car. 'I'll see you around teatime. Come and surprise me, why don't you?' He paused as he reopened the door, the rain pattering down and slicking his hair down across his face. He turned back.

The look said more than any words ever could.

Then he was into the car, buckling up as Mr Hancock pulled a U-turn and manoeuvred past the parking ambulance. Dougie placed his hand on the window, fingers splayed Spock-style in a Vulcan salute, then he was gone. I stood alone, my throat tightening. This was it. The stabilisers were off. The water wings had been thrown away. I was on my own.

I felt sick.

The back doors of the ambulance flew open as a paramedic reached in, helping his colleague haul the trolley out from within. A young woman lay upon the bed, her body juddering as the wheels sprang out from beneath the gurney and hit the floor with a clatter. Her red hair clung to her face, matted dark and sticky, her face pale and white. I stood back as the two green-suited figures rushed past, met by doctors and nurses, their voices concerned as they vanished into the A&E. I watched them go, the ambulance deserted bar a driver in the cab.

My chest was all a-tremble, leaving me lost in the moment of drama. This was going to take some getting used to. I looked into the back of the ambulance. Towards her.

The redhead inched closer, her alabaster skin shining with a familiar blue light. She looked left and right out of the back of the vehicle, as if afraid to take that first step out. From the look on her face she was confused, struggling to make sense of the world around her. My heart shuddered as the memories of my own death came flooding back, submerging me in a fleeting moment of sorrow. Then it was gone, put behind me, my own sorry story the least of my concerns. I extended a hand toward her and at that moment she saw me, flinching fearfully, face wracked by doubt. I smiled.

'The name's Will Underwood,' I said, and beckoned her down the steps towards me. 'I'm here to help.'